A Bullet for Miss Rose

Shamed by the exploits of his outlaw father, Texas Ranger Parker Burden can't ignore a case like the one he finds in the dusty town of Terlingua. In the aftermath of a bank robbery the young schoolmistress, Rose Morrison, lies dead. Assigned to pursue her killer, Parker learns that the chief suspect is the rebel son of his old friend, Mexican rancher Don Vicente Hernandez.

Teaming up with a Pinkerton detective hired to retrieve the stolen gold, Parker pursues Angel Hernandez to Mexico, shadowed by a ruthless band of bounty hunters with their own agenda. Across the border they become mixed up with the tyrannical General Ortega and uncover a sinister land-grab conspiracy.

The manhunt ends in a bloody showdown, but has Parker found the man who fired the fatal bullet at Miss Rose? And will he live long enough to find out?

A Bullet for Miss Rose

Scott Dingley

A Black Horse Western

ROBERT HALE · LONDON

ISBN 0 7090 7575 8

Robert Hale Limited
Clerkenwell House
Clerkenwell Green
London EC1R 0HT

Typeset by
Derek Doyle & Associates, Liverpool.
Printed and bound in Great Britain by
Antony Rowe Limited, Wiltshire

For Maggie

ONE

The dead Mexican was slumped in a cheap coffin that stood upright on the front porch of the Running Elk hardware store. His hands were crossed at the wrists and his mouth gasped for a final, endless breath. It was a damn crude exhibition, no matter the man's crimes. That was the way Parker Burden saw it anyway. *Surely death was punishment enough,* he thought.

The first he had seen of the dusty border town of Terlingua had been its main street, stretching out towards what he knew to be the gallows uptown. As the burning southern Texas sun beat down on him that day, Parker was not destined for the noose. He was no killer, not as a rule. Parker *was* a mystery; he was thirty years old, maybe a year or two older – he didn't know for sure. His green-blue eyes betrayed no secrets but anyone who looked into them knew they'd seen enough adventures for a dozen dime novels all the same. On this adventure he had grown a rough beard and hadn't

yet decided whether to keep it. Right now Parker
just looked forward to a bathtub and a soft bed.
For his arrival Parker had dug a white shirt out of
his *maleta* saddle-bag, tied a ribbon at the neck
and dusted off his *vaquero*'s jacket. On to this he
had pinned the silver star of a Texas Ranger. He
held the rank of sergeant and, though tousled by
the elements, you could tell Parker Burden was on
the right side of the law.

Death, in some ugly shape, always accompanied
Parker on these crossings and as he rode into
Terlingua he found that it was one step ahead of
him. Along the yellow dust track of the main street,
Parker saw the dead Mexican on display. The
scene remained with Parker, troubling him even
after he had passed it by. It brought to brutal reality a tobacco-coloured newspaper cutting that he
hoarded in his saddle-bag like a penny snatched
from circulation. On those rare occasions when he
might be drunk or melancholy enough, Parker
would gently unfold the page and see his father's
photograph. There was Joseph Burden, captured
for eternity, slumped lifeless like a waxwork
dummy in a wooden coffin. He too was propped
up in front of a store, three black holes dotting his
chest. The cutting was seven years old, the date at
the top of the page recording the exact day. Parker
didn't remember his old man too well now. In the
aftermath of the Civil War, he had found himself
on the wrong side of the law. There was no transition between Lone Star raider and long rider for

Burden senior. The war only ended when a guard killed him as he robbed a bank.

Parker brought his horse to a standstill outside the timber porch of the local jailhouse. He swung down from his mount and secured its reins on the hitching post before stepping up on to the veranda. The marshal was an old friend but it was the fact that official orders awaited Parker in Terlingua that had brought him to the god-forsaken town.

'Sleeping on the job, Marshal?' Parker said with a smile.

Walter McOwen sat dozing like an old dog, a shotgun resting across his lap.

'There's life in me yet, junior.' The muffled words came from under the marshal's Stetson, tilted down over his face. He pushed up the brim with a finger, revealing watery blue eyes. 'Want to go a few rounds, kid?'

'Not a chance, Walt.'

An ugly smile broke out from beneath the marshal's waxed moustache. The old man got to his feet and wandered with Parker across the creaking planks of the porch, inside to the shade of his office.

'Who's the stiff out front?' said Parker, sitting on the edge of the marshal's solid wooden desk and cocking a thumb back up the main street towards the dead Mexican. 'Unless he's for sale, that wretch belongs in the ground.'

The marshal stowed his shotgun in a rack

behind the desk and reluctantly answered.

'A little trouble rode into town a few days back. . . .' He was dodging the topic, almost squirming. When the marshal turned to face Parker, the old man saw he was hooked.

'Kind of trouble, Walt?'

'I tried to round up a posse but, well . . .' The marshal's voice trailed away into a sigh as he twirled one tip of his grand moustache. 'Fella in the box out there was lynched by the good folks I'm sworn to protect. Couple of days ago, a Mexicano gang stormed in to rob the bank safe. They shot young Rose Morrison, the schoolmistress. A fine lady, daughter of a Methodist minister and engaged to be married to a math teacher over at her little schoolhouse.' The marshal was shaking his head, helpless.

'She died?' Parker asked bitterly, knowing the answer.

The response came weakly.

'She died.'

The hot bath had made Parker feel half-way towards human again. For weeks on end during these manhunts he lived off the untamed and hostile plains and deserts, lived like an animal. The barber's straight razor had just finished scraping the last patch of thick beard from Parker's jaw when a tall, well-dressed man of fifty or so years stepped inside the shop, the little bell over the door heralding his entrance. He removed his hat and took a waiting seat behind Parker. The two men made eye contact in the mirrored wall. The barber spoke first,

'Afternoon, Mr Mayor, sir.'

'Louis.' It was a subdued, bored acknowledgement before a more enthusiastic one to the customer in the barber's chair: 'Parker Burden?'

Parker nodded, then spoke with deliberate insolence.

'Are you Meyer with two 'E's' or mayor with two horses and a nice big house?'

'Didn't vote for me, huh?' said the man. 'Never mind. My name's Nelson Buchanan, mayor of Terlingua. Got a nice big house for Mrs Buchanan, three or four horses as it happens, and I've got a heinous crime against the people of this town that's like a burr under my goddamn saddle.' Buchanan was agitated already, his face reddening.

'I'm sorry about Miss Morrison, she had no business dying,' said Parker, this time with sincerity.

Buchanan reached into his inside jacket pocket and withdrew a folded sheet of paper. He opened it out and held it up to Parker.

'I've got papers here signed by your commanding officer, Ranger. Official orders for you. They say you're to apprehend her killer. Forthwith.'

Parker reached for the warrant, glanced over it and stowed it away under the cape the barber had thrown over him.

'Your voters took revenge by taking the law into their own hands,' Parker said.

'Those bean-eaters tore up my town, emptied the bank vault and shot down that little lady in cold blood,' spat Buchanan. 'Four of them got clean away. Isn't that offence "offensive" enough for you, peace officer?'

Parker wiped the last of the shaving foam from his face with a clean towel, then spun the chair around to face Mayor Buchanan.

'Maybe if the "bean-eater" you caught hadn't been strung up in the street,' Parker said, 'we'd have got a lead on who his four buddies were.'

Buchanan let out a roar of laughter and clapped his fat hands together.

'We've got that covered, Ranger. The ringleader and the man who killed Miss Morrison is a desperado name of Angel Hernandez. His father has a ranch fifteen miles out of town. We'll assemble a posse in no time to run him down. What do you say?'

Parker sat forward in his chair, shaking his head. He knew what he was hearing was more persecution. The town wanted a scapegoat for the Morrison girl's death and Hernandez fitted the bill.

'I know Don Vicente Hernandez, he's no outlaw,' Parker said. 'Neither is his son. He's just a kid.'

Buchanan stared into Parker's eyes, fists clenched tightly. 'We have upstanding eye-witnesses who'll stand up in court and identify Angel. The lynched man was a ranch hand at the

Hernandez place too. Work it out yourself, Ranger.'

Parker stood from the barber's chair and dropped a few coins from his pocket on to the empty leather seat. His gaze moved from the coins to Buchanan.

'I will, Mr Mayor. That's what the politicians in Washington pay me for, isn't it?'

As Parker walked out the front door, the little bell ringing as he went, he felt sure the upstanding Mayor Buchanan was turning the air blue cursing behind his back.

Being handed assignments like this was the worst part of the job in Parker's book. It wasn't just that *this* one was personal. Parker had become a lone wolf. He had ridden in a unit of Texas Rangers under Captain George Ross Barclay and when bandits shot Barclay dead down in Nueva Rosita, Parker shunned a promotion and got permission from the governor to work manhunts solo. It was dangerous and unconventional, but it was how Parker liked to work. The establishment knew that Parker was a valuable tool and indulged him, even if they didn't understand him.

Six stores down from the barbershop was the Terlingua Savings Bank. Parker made the short walk down the main street and stopped to view the clapboard façade, tipping his Stetson to a lady pushing a baby-cart. He climbed the steps and peered in through a narrow gap in the curtained window. From the veranda beside him, a boy's voice was directed up at Parker.

'Opening an account?' the shrill voice enquired. Parker looked down at the boy who sat by the door of the bank, a carved wooden pistol in his hands and a bent tin star made by the blacksmith pinned to his shirtfront. The boy frowned so as to look official.

'I'm the bank guard, on account of the recent stick-up.'

Parker nodded, impressed.

'Good job, too,' he said, before holding aside his overcoat lapel and revealing the silver encircled star of a sworn-in Texas Ranger. The boy's eyes widened in admiration and he stood up to attention.

'You investigating teacher's murder?'

'Did you see it?'

'Sure,' the boy said enthusiastically. 'Bunch of Mexicans galloped in and came up these very steps and in that very door.' The boy began to re-enact the robbery excitedly, the carved pistol in his hand. '*Bang! Bang!*'

'What happened to the man they hanged?' Parker raised his voice to settle the boy.

'Someone shot his horse, he got left behind when the others rode out.'

'And your teacher?' Parker said carefully.

'She was running 'cross the street to see if anyone was hurt in the bank, they fired back from yonder and she got hit in the belly. Fell and died

14

right there.' The boy pointed with the pistol to a patch of dirt in front of the bank.

'You saw that too?' asked Parker, concerned.

'Yesiree,' replied the boy, once again standing to attention. Parker looked out of the town to the trail along which the boy claimed the robbers had escaped. He scanned the route all the way back to the spot where Rose Morrison had fallen. Deliberate or not, it was a murder committed in the act of an armed robbery, he thought. The man responsible should be brought to justice. But Parker could not believe that man was the son and heir of his old friend, Don Vicente. Parker had the sensation of being watched again. He scanned the street and found a mean-looking *hombre* staring across at him. The man was heavily built, with a wiry beard and wearing a distinctive long duster coat. He was staring Parker down, sizing him up, with no attempt to be inconspicuous. With one hand on the revolver in his cartridge belt, and the other holding a pipe to his ugly mouth, the man nodded to Parker as a greeting. Parker returned the hawklike stare skilfully for a few seconds.

'What's the name of that ugly rattlesnake across the street?' asked Parker.

The boy looked, shielding his eyes from the sun.

'That's Boggs. Pa says he's a troubleshooter.'

'That so?' said Parker, curious.

Parker stared at Boggs for a while longer, then looked up at the wooden frame of the veranda over the boy's head. There he saw the scorched, splintered mess of a bullet hole. Parker recognized it as a rifle round. He stepped towards it, taking out his folding pocket-knife and using the blade to dig away at the fibres of the wood. Holding his palm out flat beneath the hole, Parker extricated a mushroomed nugget of metal. He held the bullet out for the boy to see.

'Know what a repeating rifle is, kid?'

'Sure I do,' the boy replied.

'Any of them Mexicans carrying repeating rifles?'

'I dunno,' said the boy, quizzically. 'Six-shooters I reckon.'

The boy made a grab for the bullet but Parker closed his fist around it.

'Evidence, kid.'

TWO

Parker Burden hated victims like Rose Morrison.
He didn't hate *her*, for she was as pure as Montana
snow. What he hated was the way they got their
little steel hooks into the eyelets of his brain. He
hated their memory and he hated that in places
like Terlingua innocence could be ravaged and
desecrated and life – cheap life at that – just went
on. Now he was only making matters worse,
embracing the outrage of it all like he always did.
It was the true meaning of wearing a tin star, one
that the kid didn't yet understand.

With the twisted bullet tucked away in his
pocket, Parker made the short ride out to the little
wooden schoolhouse. He saw the whitewashed
bell-tower first and felt it calling to him, though
there was no justified reason for the journey.
There was no call to gain insight into Rose
Morrison the woman, she had simply been in the
wrong place at the wrong time and had died as a
result. This journey was ritual, not procedure.

Parker spotted the man he was looking for from

some distance. He was herding a dozen children dressed in smocks and suits into the schoolhouse. He looked up and saw Parker approaching. It was Rose's fiancé, a Swedish immigrant named Ike Dockweiler.

Minutes later the children had organized themselves at little desks, chalking sums on slates before a large, embroidered state flag of Texas. Their teacher was absent, speaking to the stranger outside. Some of the more curious kids neglected their work and instead watched the two men talk under the shade of a large pecan tree. They knew Mr Dockweiler had changed since Miss Morrison had gone.

Ike, a sandy-haired, softly spoken man with a faint accent, held out the pocket portrait of Rose which he now treasured. She was young and beautiful and Parker didn't care to look into her eyes for more than a passing moment.

'They say they know the man who killed my Rose. Is that right?'

'They may do, I don't. Not yet,' Parker replied.

'Whoever did it is evil. They should be made to pay. It's not enough to hang him.' Ike was losing his composure, pounding the tree trunk with a fist. He was a mild man with no sense of how to deal with the strange desire for revenge he suddenly felt.

'Do you hear me, Mr Burden? It's not enough.'

Ike reached for Parker's .44 Colt Frontier and drew it reversed from the belt holster. Parker saw it coming and could have stopped him, but he let the teacher make his point. With the revolver in his hand, Ike postured and enjoyed the power he felt. He cocked the hammer awkwardly, the first time he had done it in his life.

'I'll do it myself. *I'll* find him and *I'll* kill him. I'll put a bullet in *his* belly, see if *he* likes it. . . .'

Parker had heard enough. He locked his hand around the teacher's wrist and squeezed hard. Ike yelped and dropped the revolver into Parker's other hand, which hovered ready below.

'Sure you will, Ike,' Parker said as he reholstered his revolver. 'You'll kill him slowly with algebra, and fractions and long multiplication.'

Ike began to weep into his hands. Parker watched as he slumped to his knees beneath the big tree, sobbing like a baby. The more curious kids in the schoolhouse saw it all too.

'Damn them,' Parker thought as he turned back to his horse, 'it's these Terlingua tragedies that are the *real* killers.'

Parker would have to ride out to the Hernandez ranch and see whether the smoke of accusations had any spark of truth. He hoped to God they did not. It was too late now and his horse had travelled far enough for one day. Rose could wait.

Parker had rented a room for the night above Kitty's saloon, bang in the middle of the main street. The room was small and its decoration a little feminine for Parker's taste, but that very quality somehow made it comforting to him.

Parker sat on the edge of the bed facing a flowery-papered wall, scrutinizing his reflection in a fancy egg-shaped looking-glass. He still looked young for a man of thirty, though the outside corners of his eyes were creased from squinting. He wore his dark hair a little too long and when his beard grew it came out reddish – a legacy from his Scottish grandparents.

He shifted focus to the window behind him in the reflection, noticing the pink-orange sunset already streaking across the sky. From downstairs he heard the saloon's mechanical pianola play its tinny tunes. Tonight Parker intended to share a few drinks with the marshal, talk shop, and get some sleep in a comfortable bed before beginning the usual routine of taking on a new assignment. He would have enjoyed a jaunt to a larger town nearby, to sample more comfortable beds and more hot baths and wet shaves that weren't interrupted by furious town officials. But here he was in the quicksand of Terlingua, caught between the dead Rose Morrison and the condemned Angel Hernandez. Parker stared into his own eyes again, then glanced at the bullet from the bank, now resting on a lace doily on top of a cabinet with brass handles. He ran a hand wearily through his slicked-back hair, before heading for the door.

Downstairs in the saloon, Marshal McOwen was already propping up the bar when Parker stepped out of his room. He was smoking a pipe and was a little drunk as he cooed over the legendary Kitty

Madigan, who held court there every night with singsongs and coarse jokes. The marshal spotted Parker half-way down the staircase and raised his glass.

'Parker Burden, c'mon and fill your glass. Or should I say empty it?'

'Evening, Walt, Kitty.' Parker nodded as whiskey was splashed from an unlabelled bottle into his glass. He drank it down and promptly placed the empty vessel on the bar.

The marshal laughed, 'You're playing catch up, sonny.'

Parker gave a wry little smile, 'That's my life story, Walt.'

Not tonight, Parker thought. One or two gulps of Kitty's mystery pop-skull and that would be his fill. He wasn't a hard drinker like the marshal; wasn't a gambler either. In fact, Parker had no vices to speak of, only that dogged determination to see justice done. Not that he was a religious man or one who followed the rule of law blindly. It was a hang-up, a chip on his shoulder that caused him no end of trouble.

Parker and the marshal took a table in the centre of the saloon and now sat facing one another, huddled up in conversation. The marshal still nursed the whiskey bottle that Parker had long since given up on. He always drank plenty the night before a hanging.

'I'll ride out and talk to Don Vicente tomorrow, clear up this business,' said Parker.

'And if Angel really is guilty?' asked the marshal.

'We'll see.'

' "We" is right. I hear the bank have hired a detective to find their gold,' said the marshal. 'One of them Pinkerton fellows from St Louis or New York or someplace.'

Parker frowned as the marshal continued: 'He's coming in on the stage tomorrow and he won't have any bias towards Angel.'

'If Angel's guilty, he's guilty. I've got my official orders,' said Parker, brooding. He did not welcome the prospect of a big-city detective from the East shadowing him with his Yankee deportment and his textbook police theories.

As Parker was chewing over his misfortune, a red-faced drunk came wheeling towards their table, his starched collar loose and pointing up to the ceiling. Parker remembered seeing him at the bar when he checked in hours ago. The marshal sat back and gave his full attention to the clown, who slammed a half-empty glass down between them.

'What in the hell are you doing making merry when poor Rose's no-good killers are out there?' he slurred.

'Come on now, Chester, we're doing all we can,' said the marshal, unconvincingly.

'Like hell you are. Send for all the Pinkertons and Texas Rangers you please to, we know who done it. Maybe we should just throw another lynching for that Hernandez dog.'

That just about did it for Parker. He shot to his feet, toppling his chair and surprising the drunk who stood some three or four inches shorter than he.

'Not another word, *borracho*.' Fury was burning red in Parker's eyes.

'Who are you calling drunk?' said Chester, his eyes red too but not from fury.

At the bar ahead of Parker, the man in the duster, Boggs, was present and now let his hand fall on to his holstered revolver. *How long has he been tailing me and why?* Parker wondered. Parker reached for his revolver and drew it half an inch out of its holster.

'Watch your back, Ranger,' said Boggs. 'A lot of people is itching for payback.'

The man sneered and Parker's eyes darted around the room, assessing the potential stand-off.

Around the saloon he picked out more and more of the same buff-coloured dusters; to his left, right and even at the pianola behind him. There were perhaps six in all, making it a hopeless situation. He let the six-shooter slip back down to rest.

Boggs spoke up again. 'The drunk makes sense,' he said. 'What's keeping you from hunting that mad dog down?'

'The law, until it *proves* the accused is guilty,' Parker responded in a booming voice.

'And I hear tell you're mighty friendly with the accused.' Boggs spat the last word out like snake venom. Parker continued, addressing all those in the saloon now.

'Tomorrow morning I'll be riding out solo to find Angel Hernandez, the boy suspected of the crimes you're all riled about. I'll do it as a sworn-in representative of the law. That means no lynching, no hired guns, and no speaking out of turn to the good marshal here.'

Chester backed away unsteadily to the bar, while Boggs let the flap of his duster fall back over his *buscadero* gunbelt, covering the revolver and the two sheath knives tucked alongside it.

'Maybe the bank's Pinkerton man will sniff out some incriminating clues, help you do your proving.' The saloon erupted into laughter and Boggs, mighty pleased with himself, turned his back on Parker. The marshal gestured to sit and Parker eventually descended to his chair. Slowly the tension around the room eased, and the normal atmosphere of chatter and bad pianola music returned. Parker, however, still fumed.

'Who are the hoodlums in the long coats, anyway, Walt? Why so many?' he asked.

'They're the "Regulators",' answered the marshal. 'They work for Theodore Mulhearn, the big cattle rancher. They solve his problems.'

'Mercenaries,' said Parker.

The marshal nodded. 'You know who the boss Regulator is?'

Parker tilted his head, curious.

'Only "Bloody Bill" Logan, that's who.'

For all its sprung cushioning and fine feathers,

that comfortable bed Parker had so longed for didn't do him a bit of good. He might as well have been out under the stars by a camp-fire, because proper sleep eluded him the whole damned night. Partly it was because the bed was a foot too short for his stature, but it was the haunting visions of a lifetime of ghosts that plagued his restless mind worst of all. There in the oval looking-glass at the foot of the bed he swore he could see poor, beautiful Rose Morrison pleading with him. Then the face was that of the broken Ike Dockweiler, sobbing and vowing vengeance; Angel Hernandez appeared as the lynched coffin-man, who seemed to blur into Parker's wayward father. When a church bell rang somewhere in the distance, Parker realized it was morning. He knew that Rose Morrison's murderer had to be punished, otherwise the ghosts in the mirror wouldn't ever let him sleep soundly.

THREE

El Monje the locals called him. It meant the monk and it was an affectionate dig at his honorable nature and simple way of life. Parker had known Don Vicente Hernandez for many years and knew the moniker was appropriate. Granted, there were inconsistencies with this humble image: the wealthy Mexican-American rancher had built up his herd and lands from nothing, and he appreciated his position among the powerful élite. The myriad Hernandez offspring could have made the *El Monje* tag seem ironic too, of course. He'd fathered around seventeen children, twelve of whom survived. Most lived at the hacienda, including his son, the rebellious eighteen-year-old Angel.

Parker liked to think of Don Vicente as a surrogate father too. Twice or three times a year he would still make the journey out to the Hernandez ranch, usually taking with him gifts for Don Vicente and his wife. But it had been a while since Parker had been able to visit and he had since heard that the *señora* had died of typhoid that past fall. There would be no gifts on this unhappy outing.

Parker had readied his horse and packed up water and chow early so as to slip out of town unnoticed. He hoped that at last night's showdown he had staked his claim boldly and would satisfy the citizens of Terlingua, who still smarted from the audacious but tragic raid. It was only some fifteen miles out to the Hernandez ranch, but long before it appeared on the horizon Parker saw a thick plume of black smoke smudging the sky. The veins on either side of his neck throbbed red hot as Parker first thought the hacienda itself was ablaze. Riding hard and fast, he soon came across the actual source of the fire – a barn on the outskirts of the homestead, left skeletal, black and smouldering. The blaze had done its worst and now a dozen exhausted ranch hands were moseying back home carrying empty buckets. As Parker rode among them he called out in Mexican:

'Where is *El Monje*?'

A young cowboy saw Parker's tin star glint in the sun, then lifted his bucket wearily and gestured straight ahead to the ranch.

'He rode back already, what can we do against the Regulators?' he replied.

Parker gripped the reins tighter and spurred his horse on towards the ranch.

Little Esperanza Hernandez had pointed behind the hacienda and cried '*Mamá*' when Parker asked for her father. At first he thought to correct her but then caught up with the child's logic. He continued past, towering above her on his mount, until he had cleared the side of the main building and his old friend came into view. Dressed in a white linen suit and hat, Don Vicente stood with his head bowed and hands clasped tightly to his chest, looking very much like a man named *El Monje*. Before him was a small square formed by a picket fence, inside which Parker could just see the tip of a fine gravestone. *Of course* Esperanza's father was with her mother, he thought.

At the moment Parker prompted his horse to trot forward, Don Vicente looked up and saw him. The blur of tears made him fearful of the stranger for a brief moment, until he recognized Parker and a smile broke out on his face. Parker climbed down from his horse and walked towards Don Vicente, his right hand extended for a greeting. The Mexican smiled and held open both his arms, embracing Parker and patting his back firmly.

'My old friend Parker,' he said. 'Why so long?'

Parker shrugged having no excuse other than life itself.

'You heard about my wife?' Don Vicente gestured to the grave, then took Parker by the arm and led him to it. 'The doctor could do nothing for her. She was a good woman, no?'

'She surely was,' Parker agreed, a bitter smile on his lips. He slipped the hat from his head and looked down at the grave, remembering. There was silence, before . . .

'You're having trouble from Theodore Mulhearn?' Parker asked.

'Yes,' admitted Don Vicente, somehow ashamed. 'Today they burned down my barn. Maybe tomorrow they will burn down my home and my children.'

'What's their quarrel?' asked Parker, 'Land or livestock?'

Don Vicente had become embroiled in an escalating war with neighbouring Anglo ranchers over the ownership of stray cattle. Theodore Mulhearn was the richest and most powerful of them: a big-sugar cattleman above the law who could frame and kill innocent settlers as rustlers, and raid Hispanic ranchitos without reprisal. It would only be a matter of time before Mulhearn's hired guns spilled blood at the Hernandez ranch.

Don Vicente looked up at Parker sadly. 'I do not wish to see any more death in my home, Parker,' he said.

The dispute with Mulhearn and his so-called Regulators was of personal interest, but Parker could not forget he was here on official business. The subject of Angel and his role in the death of Rose Morrison would have to be raised, no matter how difficult. Don Vicente had invited Parker to drink *tinto* wine on the shaded veranda of his hacienda. The tall glass of wine cleared the dust from Parker's throat and made him dizzy enough to broach Angel's name. Don Vicente, who sat with his daughter Esperanza on his knee, was at first reluctant.

'My son rode away with three men, they went south. He told me he had struck a blow against the men who persecute us. I knew then my son was in trouble.'

'You were right,' said Parker. 'He's been accused of emptying the Terlingua bank, along with four other men. One died in town. That leaves three with him.'

Don Vicente buried his face in the oblivious Esperanza's back.

'Now my son,' he said mournfully. 'He had become concerned by the plight of his people, Latinos.'

'Tell me where he was headed and I'll try to protect him,' said Parker. 'I'm probably his best guardian, after his god, that is.'

Don Vicente stood, set Esperanza down, and walked through the white muslin curtains which danced over the doorway into his study. When he returned, he handed Parker a large money-sack. It was empty and folded, but the stenciled words *Bank of Terlingua* were visible on the front of the thick canvas.

'*Gracias*, Don Vicente.'

'I know I can trust you to do what is right,' Don Vicente said. 'He asked a ranch hand to burn this before heading south to El Carricito.'

Parker nodded and set the bag on the table.

'Then you should burn it,' he said.

A petite young Mexican woman wearing a corseted lemon-yellow dress approached the table with a pitcher full of wine and refilled their glasses. Parker looked up at her and she smiled softly back. This was Don Vicente's most beautiful achievement, Parker thought. Like her father, old *El Monje*, her name was fitting too.

'Inmaculada, my sweet,' Don Vicente said. 'Tonight you will sing beautiful words of romance and longing for our guest.'

Don Vicente's eldest daughter had her mother's good looks and her father's sweet nature. Her face was tanned and her almond-shaped eyes were the same raven-black as her silky hair, framed by long lashes and topped by fine, arching brows. Her lips were full and pink and seemed to smile as a rule. She laughed, then spun around and walked gracefully away along the veranda. Inmaculada's all too fleeting presence left a hollow feeling in Parker's heart. He wanted to follow her. But as he sipped the now sickly-sweet wine and breathed the dying scent of her French perfume, he settled for cursing the twist of fate that had brought him here bearing a gun instead of gifts.

The evenings out at the hacienda could be charming or oppressive. For Parker, they were a little of both; there was the beauty of Inmaculada and her Spanish ballads, but the incessant chatter of those unseen cicadas was like a ticking pocket-watch, reminding him that his future would be bonded with the fugitive Angel's. Don Vicente too knew that he could soon lose a son, be it his flesh and blood or the young Ranger he cared deeply for.

Parker had decided to see the sun set at his spiritual home one more time before the manhunt to El Carricito. They gathered in the drawing-room and Inmaculada sang many *corrido* folk songs with heart-rending lyrics while one of her brothers played guitar. Her last song was just for Parker, he knew it by the way her dark eyes constantly met his. She sang of how her heart broke when he left her, and Parker made a promise to himself that after this assignment she wouldn't ever have to sing the words again. Then Parker wondered whether she knew the truth about his presence at the ranch and the fantasy of the lyrics was shattered.

Inmaculada retired to her room while Parker and her father smoked cigars and sipped brandy. She sat at an ornate vanity unit, combing her long black hair and humming the melody to Parker's ballad. Inmaculada was shrewd and quick-witted like her father, she had known exactly why Parker had come the minute she set eyes on him. Like her father, Inmaculada accepted that Angel was a passionate *mesteño*, a wild young stallion that could not be broken. Of course, there were consequences to that. Something terrible could easily happen to the tall, handsome American down in Mexico too, so when she prayed for Angel's safe return she also mentioned Parker.

When he walked sleepily towards the guest

bedroom late that night, Parker had no idea he was in Inmaculada's thoughts. In fact, he felt an overwhelming sadness and was compelled to take out the yellowed news-cutting to read. It could only ever make him feel worse and he knew it. He had read only three lines of the words Parker knew by heart when there came the jolting sound of gunfire from outside. Parker listened, his head a little dizzy from the liquor. Five rounds fired in succession, then the sound of a woman's tormented cry. The warm glow of oil-burning lamps soon filled the previously dormant homestead, as ranchers were roused from sleep. Parker dropped the cutting, grabbed his revolver from its belt holster hanging on the back of a chair, and bolted out the door.

Beyond the veranda, a ranch hand was slumped in the arms of a portly woman whom Parker knew to be the children's nanny. He had a bullet wound in his thigh that bled profusely into the dust. Don Vicente appeared wide-eyed from the house, wearing a robe, while Inmaculada was cuddling a frightened Esperanza in the doorway.

'Get back inside,' yelled Parker as he rushed towards the wounded man. 'Put a tourniquet on that leg,' he instructed the nanny. Parker grabbed a burning torch from another cowboy and ran with the six-shooter in his other hand, out into the night. His heart was beating hard in his chest as he swung the flame around to illuminate the consuming darkness. Just as he became breathless, the sound of a horse's hoofs made Parker stop dead. The cicadas had gone eerily silent. Parker trained his gun towards the noise and threw the still-blazing torch stick out into the darkness with a whoosh of licking flames. As it fell to the dust, the torch illuminated first the legs of a bolting horse and then its rider. The horse was controlled skilfully before the rider turned his back on Parker and, aiming over his shoulder, fired a single shot into the air over Parker's head. The gunpowder smoke-cloud rose towards the stars, and the man was gone in a charge. Parker fired the revolver into the night after him until the hammer struck an empty chamber. Parker knew who he was even in the flickering orange light and black shadows, and he knew that the man had escaped unharmed. It was Bill Logan who had spilled the first blood.

When Parker returned to Terlingua the next morning, a few expectant people wanted to know where the hell Angel was. He wasn't sure what to do about Bill Logan and his criminal Regulators, but the thought of Don Vicente and his family at their mercy enraged and alarmed Parker. He was beginning to understand the citizens' desire for a forthright lynching. Parker had only come back here to stock up on the necessary provisions at the trading-post. He would take the journey slowly, he thought, changing horse along the way if necessary, bedding down in the little pueblo settlements on both sides of the Rio Grande. He wouldn't wear his tin star and the fact that he spoke Spanish fluently would aid him in his mission.

The store was run by an old man wearing a white apron who looked half-Indian, and it was packed to the rafters with every item that could conceivably be bought or bartered: from woven Navajo blankets to rainbow-coloured gumballs. The old man had an impressive array of short and long firearms too, advertised by the big carved revolver sign that hung over the doorway. Extra guns would not be needed on this crossing, at least Parker hoped not.

As the Ranger loaded the store counter with tinware, dried meat and blankets, another new arrival to Terlingua was causing a stir of his own. A Concord stagecoach had pulled into town and as soon as the bruised travellers inside had touched firm ground they shuffled off with their luggage in the direction of Kitty's saloon. One man was in less of a hurry though. He simply removed his derby hat and gazed up at the scorching sun, breathing deeply and with a slight smile, until the coachman threw his leather travelling bag down from the roof into the dust. His name, confirmed by the embossed lettering on the soiled bag, was G.W. Dooley, and he'd been journeying by road and rail from the city of New York for what seemed an eternity. Gawking Terlingua locals could see just from his highfalutin' threads that the stranger was from back East. Dooley's plan was to rent a room, preferably at a respectable boarding-house run by a widow rather than at the popular saloon across the street. He would rest up a while, bathe, then purchase a repeating rifle and a handgun, preferably a reliable Remington .45. Dooley had a little one-shot derringer in his bag among his clean shirts and long johns, but that was strictly an under-the-pillow precaution. For this case he'd need something more . . . respectable.

Before all that, Dooley thought, he must report in to the bank, for it was they who had contacted the Pinkerton detective agency and invited him all this way. The boy on the steps to the bank shot Dooley as he went past. The detective feigned death by clasping his chest and continued inside, laughing. The bank's interior was small and dark. Dooley set his travelling bag down on the floor.

'Dooley of the Pinkerton Agency, New York office,' he said loudly to the frail clerk behind the counter. 'Manager about?'

The clerk took a pencil out of his mouth and ambled away for a moment, leaving Dooley alone to tap his fingers on the counter and look around at the deficient security of the bank. He heard a shrill voice address him and turned to face it.

'Detective Dooley, is it?' the voice asked.

The bank-manager was a tall, grey-haired man in a frock-coat, very efficient-looking. If the bank's board of executives wanted their stolen gold back, this fellow was eager to save face.

'You'd better come through to my office,' said the manager. 'Mayor Buchanan is waiting there.'

*

Parker had paid for his kit and had carried it all wrapped in the Navajo blankets out to the stables behind the saloon. His horse had been fed and watered since his return from the hacienda and he wanted to set out straight away while the light was still good. He knew of a little adobe ruin where he could bed down tonight, then set off again at first light tomorrow. Thus it was back to being a predator and living like an animal. Piece by piece, Parker stowed the equipment away in bedrolls and saddle-bags. When the last of it was away he picked up the saddle-blankets, shook off the straw pieces, and began to fold them.

The sequence of events that followed happened fast, overwhelming Parker. He felt a blow to the back of his head, followed by the scrape of the blanket's rough texture against his face. *Focus*, he willed himself. *Stay . . . awake . . . .*

He could hear the shuffle of footsteps on the straw littered floor . . .

The cocking of a gun hammer . . .

Parker fought off the feeling of sinking into a deep, inklike well of blackness, desperately trying to draw his six-shooter. He collapsed to the floor of the stable, rolled around on his back, then withdrew underneath his horse. His revolver was free and his limp hand squeezed off a round that punched uselessly into a timber beam. The man who had struck him laughed and slowly came into focus.

'Boggs.'

A gunshot rang out as Parker succumbed to unconsciousness.

Boggs had heard what Parker hadn't. It was a softly spoken 'Hey' that made him turn slightly, his six-shooter leading the way. When Dooley saw the dull glint of gun metal, he fired without hesitation. The tiny, pearl-handled silver derringer was so small it took a moment for Boggs even to realize he'd been shot, but when he did the big man slumped to the ground like a sack full of cannon-balls. Parker came to quickly, unsure of whether he was still of this earth. The revolver was still heavy in his hand and straw pieces were clinging to his clothes and hair. His bleary eyes gradually focused on a well-dressed gentleman of big-city appearance standing behind him where the blow had been delivered. The gentleman held a travelling-bag in one hand, a derringer pistol in the other. Parker instinctively lifted his six-shooter and Dooley spoke out, hands held up in surrender.

'Easy, Ranger. I'm not the cad who slugged you.' Dooley pointed down to Boggs, who lay dead on the stable floor alongside the groggy Parker. On his shirtfront, over the heart, was a tiny red dot. 'I was coming to collect my horse and saw him about to blow your brains out, thought I'd intervene,' explained Dooley. 'I'm glad I did now I see you're a lawman.'

He helped Parker to his feet and dusted him off.

'Lucky the one bullet put him down, a big bear like that.'

Parker looked down at the dead man.

'My name's G.W. Dooley,' the newcomer announced. 'I'm a Pinkerton agent sent out here to solve a bank robbery and to find the culprit.' Dooley handed Parker a business card with, Parker saw, a printed picture of an eye and the words *We Never Sleep*. Rubbing the back of his head with his other hand, Parker returned the card to Dooley who took it back with no offence.

'Thanks. We'd better get this guy to the marshal,' said Parker wearily. 'Grab his legs, I'll take this end.'

FOUR

There were *bandidos* and there were rebels; in Angel's mind the two were a world apart. This majestic land of his was teeming with greedy, murderous thieves, not just Mexicans but gringos too; they seemed to breed and spread their ills like gangrene. Angel preferred to liken their presence in Mexico to body lice on a princess. He was a rebel, not a bandit.

The loss of a good man during the Terlingua raid was hard to face, his fate at the hands of an enraged lynch mob harder still. Angel reminded himself that sacrifices would be necessary, and each of the brave rebels who shared Angel's ideal knew as much. When they robbed gold or guns to give to the peasants it was to save the lives of those who were oppressed.

With the three surviving rebels, Angel had ridden out from his father's ranch, saddles weighed down by the stolen gold. They had divided it up, five bars wrapped in sackcloth to each man. A fortune. Already, he had heard the bank officials were claiming twice as much had been stolen. That was their attempt at screwing him right back. Don Vicente's parting words had been bittersweet, but Angel was grateful for them.

You are a man now, my son, your choices are your own.

Angel remembered the words and how tears had appeared in his father's eyes. Angel loved the ranch, but by God it could be suffocating. He needed to be free and to explore the world beyond it. To do something that mattered, not just to enjoy the harvest of Don Vicente's struggles.

At the edge of the Rio Grande the rebels could look across to their homeland. Its landscape was the same as that which they now stood on – a sprawling desert of dust. But it stirred emotions in each silent man and Angel knew that he had made the right choice. The rumblings of rebellion could be heard across the plains.

There were other perils down here, especially for those carrying such valuables. The rebels' route would take them through some deadly territory. About eight miles east of Los Alamos a notorious band of robber-bandits, mostly half-breeds and mulattos, had been preying on travellers. They would appear from caves and ambush riders on the trail. Legend had it that they scalped their victims Indian-style and might even be cannibals too. Rumours spread like wildfire down here, but Angel knew the dangers of road agentry were real.

It was therefore at that stone's throw distance

from Los Alamos, exactly half-way between Terlingua and El Carricito, that a nervous Angel doubled the watchmen at night. Two men would keep guard for four-hour shifts while two slept and so on. It was Angel's turn to sleep, and he lay with his head on his saddle seat, watching the camp-fire flames through half-closed eyes. Despite willing his brain to stop working overtime, he could not be seduced by sleep. His father's words were repeating in his mind. Perhaps it was fear that kept him awake, more likely it was the pure rush of taking his destiny into his own hands. A warm breeze whipped up dust from the south and made the flames flicker and whoosh. Angel blinked his eyes and wasn't sure if the figures he saw emerging from the greasewood bushes were really there. Under the woollen saddle-blanket that now covered him, Angel's fingers crept over the revolver he had rested beside his right thigh. He kept his eyes narrowed to feign sleep, aimed the six-gun under the blanket and cocked the hammer. The nightmare figures *were* real and crept closer towards him, the fire's glow picking out the detail in their clothing and their faces. A split second before Angel fired the first shot through the saddle blanket, he saw the trophies hanging from the bandits' belts. They were human scalps.

That had all gone down four days ago.

Today's turn of events was the last thing in the

world that Parker needed. His departure would be delayed, though not by long as the dead Regulator was hurried into a coffin and up to the bone orchard with little procedure or ceremony. Worse was the fact that Parker now had a travelling companion in the gentlemanly Agent Dooley. That could drag the two-week trip out to a month. Parker didn't intend to be on the trail for that length of time. True, the man had saved his life, Parker thought, but with Dooley's task the recovery of the stolen loot, Parker knew the balance of justice had just tipped against Angel's favour.

Parker considered keeping the El Carricito lead to himself but thought better of it. The man was a private detective after all, and Parker didn't want any unnecessary anguish caused to Don Vicente's family. The bank executives had provided Dooley with a fine appaloosa horse gratis, so Parker briefed him and revealed his plan to set out right away. Dooley bemoaned the fact he wouldn't have a chance to find that respectable boarding-house, but insisted on at least spending out on some fire-power now that he'd proved he could handle a gun. Parker recommended the trading post with the wheelbarrows and axe-handles out front and held the reins of both his and Dooley's mounts while he remained outside. Half-way through whistling one of last night's ballads that had etched itself in his mind, Parker saw Ike Dockweiler steer a horse and cart into town and stop outside Kitty's. Ike looked over in Parker's direction, then disappeared through the saloon's swing-doors. Half an hour later, Dooley proudly emerged from the trading post with a Winchester rifle wrapped in brown paper, and a newly strapped-on shoulder-holster device holding a Remington revolver.

'Ain't that revolver meant to be strapped a little lower?' Parker quipped. When Dooley had replied that this was the fashion for wearing a service revolver back East, Parker knew he was in for a hell of a time.

As Parker rode out of Terlingua alongside Dooley, it was with a mixture of dread and expectation. Their departure did not go unnoticed: Ike Dockweiler staggered out from Kitty's to watch them go, frustrated that he wasn't made of Parker's mettle. Inside the saloon, through the window with fancy lettering painted on it, one of Bloody Bill Logan's Regulators watched them too. He left his poker-game straight away and fetched his own horse. He knew Logan would be mighty pleased when he reported what he'd seen.

Parker wondered whether Dooley knew about his bond to the Hernandez family. The detective seemed shrewd enough, and Parker felt certain the bank would have eagerly provided all the intelligence they could to secure their stolen gold. He had mentioned recovering the gold *and* catching the culprit, which Parker read as corporate talk for them never wanting to see Angel alive again. He also thought it was optimistic on Dooley's part. That said, within an hour of his arrival Dooley had killed a man with a precisely aimed bullet to the heart and saved Parker's life while he himself lay floundering on the stable floor like a pregnant mare. The detective was shaping up to be a mystery himself. In those first few hours in the saddle, Parker occupied his mind by running through the arrest warrant that Buchanan had pressed on him. Signed by his commanding officer from headquarters in Yselta, Texas, it charged Sergeant Parker Burden, Company D, Frontier Battalion, Texas Rangers, to apprehend Angel and escort him to the Terlingua jailhouse. The ending would be the same as with any job, he guessed: a noose for Angel if the Ranger followed orders.

As they rode on towards the Rio Grande, Dooley was absorbing all the details of the landscape. They were following the course of the Terlingua Creek which ran south from the town straight into the great river. Dooley marvelled at the great expanse of sky framed by rocky hills; the strange trees and shrubs they passed and the wildlife which occasionally passed them. He asked Parker the names of some of the cactus, like chokecherry and deerbush and ocotillo, then decided to make sketches in his notebook later and seek out the Latin names when he returned back East.

'What are all these places, haunted mansions?' Dooley asked as they passed another abandoned homestead. Its rusty windmill spun noisily while tumbleweed rolled silently across the barren ground.

'The settlers have been forced out by cattle kings,' answered Parker.

'Is that legal?'

Parker didn't answer. Of course it wasn't, but what did that matter to men like Mulhearn? They rode on until the metallic squeal of the windmill blades had faded. Before long, the lawmen found evidence of the clearances – a cattle drive crossing their path.

'There's the cause of your ghost town,' Parker shouted over the din. 'Beef.'

Dooley's pasty white face and neck took on the glow of sunburn as they rode further south. When they stopped at a pozo waterhole to refill their canteens, Dooley insisted on knowing the route they were taking. Parker took out his pocket-knife and cut a map into the dust, first a long wavy line, then points on either side of it.

'The Rio Grande snakes along and acts as the border,' he said. 'Terlingua is back here.' He poked the blade into the ground north of the line. 'Jaboncillos is here, Los Alamos here.' He made two more points south of the line. 'All the way down to El Carricito, here.'

He stuck the knife into the map up to the hilt and left it there.

'And New York . . . here.' Dooley took the knife and plunged it into the ground as far away as he could reach.

46

'And then some,' said Parker.

After they mounted up and continued on their way, Dooley was at last able to divulge some clues about himself to Parker. He was as yet unmarried, though planned to wed his sweetheart the following summer and to honeymoon on Rhode Island. He had been a constable in the New York police force until he cheated death in a shooting incident two years before and retired injured – and decorated – to join the Pinkerton agency. He had since solved some of the branch's most infamous cases, and had even had a music-hall routine dedicated to him called *Dooley's Chinatown Showdown*. Parker was growing to like him. He sensed that a gent like Dooley couldn't help but be haunted by Rose's little portrait too. Yet here they were, bound for El Carricito, on incompatible missions. Parker's motivation in setting after Angel Hernandez was to hear his side of the Rose Morrison story, perhaps also to protect him. Dooley's interest was the theft, and he was potentially the threat from whom Angel needed protection.

'What do you know about this Angel Hernandez, Dooley?' asked Parker.

'An awful lot less than you,' he replied. So the bank had told him everything, Parker thought. He could not presume to pull the wool over Dooley's eyes any more.

'I know he was involved in the robbery,' said Parker, 'but I don't have him down as a killer.'

'Did you have me down as one?' said a wry Dooley.

Parker had left the Hernandez ranch virtually defenceless and the thought of Inmaculada gunned down like Rose plagued him. Perhaps he should have disregarded his orders and let Angel find that sanctuary in Mexico, instead hunting down Bloody Bill and his Regulators. Then Rose would stay dead and Inmaculada would never know that he had ridden out to her hacienda that day for a showdown with her beloved brother. Parker did not yet know that Logan was bearing down on *him*.

The day had faded into a purple twilight by the time Parker and Dooley found the adobe ruin. It was little more than a baked-mud outhouse painted in peeling white; most of the roof had fallen in or blown away, and at some point a hog had wandered in looking for food and, finding none, had fouled on the floor instead. The land outside showed scorched and littered signs of its being used occasionally as an overnight camp by journeymen like Parker. The horses were watered and allowed to forage close by, then Parker set a camp-fire blazing and placed strips of bacon he had brought along on to a metal plate to fry. By tomorrow night, he assured Dooley, they would find a cantina in some pueblo where bread, chilli and watery beer could be purchased. For now, though, they would eat and sleep under the stars, a prospect that thrilled the city man. As they idly stoked the flames with sticks and drank coffee from battered metal cups, it was he who spoke first.

'Perhaps this Angel fellow isn't capable of calculated homicide,' said Dooley. 'Maybe it was an accident, a stray bullet?'

'Of course it's possible,' said Parker as he reached into his jacket pocket. 'But I dug this bullet out of the front of the bank. It's bent out of shape, but you can still tell it's from a rifle.' Dooley took the bullet from Parker and examined it by the light of the fire.

'So?' he said, intrigued.

'So, the robbers seemed to be carrying six-shooters, not *sixteen*-shooters,' said Parker. 'Plus,' he went on, 'the angle the bullet struck the front of the bank was high. Higher than horseback, which was where Angel was when they say he fired.'

'Interesting,' said Dooley as he handed the bullet back over the flames. 'You know, Parker, I'm a professional like you. Just because I'm a private detective doesn't make me a whore of the law as it were. A true version of events is the only conclusion I look for.'

'I appreciate that, G.W.,' said Parker with a nod.

'Granville Wulfric the second, before you ask,' Dooley said, grinning.

'That's some inheritance, Dooley,' Parker replied, laughing.

'I always wanted the "W" to stand for "Wyatt",'

said Dooley, shaking his head. The laughter faded.

'What about your folks? Texicans?' asked Dooley, still smiling.

'Both long dead,' replied Parker, staring into the flames. 'Ma had a hard face and a soft heart, and Pa was involved with the law.'

'A star-toter too?'

Parker snorted and reached over to the saddle-bags that were doubling up as his pillow. He took out the tattered news-cutting and handed it over to Dooley.

'Not our side of it,' Parker said with bitter irony.

Dooley remained silent for a few long minutes, frowning as he read the article in the flickering light.

'Good Lord, Parker,' he whispered.

Parker read the same lines in his head as Dooley saw them for the first time. His lips moved in mute recital. They read how Joseph Burden and an accomplice had entered the rural bank of Shallowater in March of 1868, carrying revolvers and dynamite, and with neckerchiefs masking their faces. How they had blown the bank safe to find its shelves empty, then found *themselves* cornered by private guards whom the bank had hired to lay ambush.

Dooley looked up at Parker and saw that he was staring blank-faced towards the stars, a million miles away in thought. His own gaze returned to the article, where he continued to read that the leader of the hired band had shown the two outlaws no mercy. They were riddled with gunfire, dragged outside and – in an unrefined postscript the otherwise hard-nosed bank executives had been a little uncomfortable with – lynched on the limb of a chaparro oak tree. The ruthless leader had then got the dead long riders documented by a travelling portrait photographer. He had received a large sum of money for his triumph, and later for his tale of derring-do. The leader even got himself a sobriquet in the journals and gazettes: they called him 'Bloody Bill'.

The distant crack and echo of gunfire broke across the landscape, making Dooley jump to his feet. Parker hardly stirred, still gazing up to the heavens.

'That was shooting, no?' Dooley asked as he looked out to the moonlit horizon.

'Ain't thunder,' Parker replied calmly. 'Settlers are moving the Comanche Indians off their land and on to the sunset trail; every once in a while the Indians fight back.'

Dooley sank slowly back to the ground.

'See that full moon?' asked Parker. 'That's a Comanche moon, perfect for raiding.'

Dooley shivered then looked back down at the ground. He had dropped the news-cutting, startled by the noise, and it now lay half curled up in flames by the camp-fire.

'Parker! Your paper, it's . . .' he shrieked, stamping on the article.

Parker slipped his hat down over his eyes and spoke, unruffled.

'Let it burn, Granville,' he said. 'Let the damn thing burn.'

FIVE

Those words, 'Let the damn thing *burn*,' must have echoed across the southern Texas plains like the sounds of the far off Comanche skirmish. A few short miles from the adobe ruin, Bloody Bill Logan had them on his mind too. Logan was a stocky man with a thick beard and blank shark's eyes that seemed too far apart, his face was grimy with a mix of trail-dirt and sweat. He sat in front of a crackling camp-fire poking at the dancing orange flames with the blade of a Bowie knife. Logan was oblivious of the fact that his bloodiest moment of glory was now going up in smoke, thanks to Dooley, but he shared the sentiment. It would be the ranch of Don Vicente Hernandez that Logan would let burn. The big man himself too, along with all his offspring including his damned son.

First though, Angel had to be brought back. It was too risky to let him get away. Logan and the three men he had chosen specially to accompany him would tail Parker and the detective across the border and straight to the fugitive young Mexican. Angel would die down south, along with the two Americans, and Logan would haul the body of Don Vicente's son back to drop on the hacienda doorstep in true Bloody Bill style, before letting the lot burn. Mr Mulhearn was paying good money to have his problems solved and it was the kind of work that suited Logan best. There was added incentive too, since Burden or the Yankee had put a bullet in Boggs. He was a good Regulator, as mean and low-down as they come. *Darn them infernal lawmen*, Logan thought.

When he withdrew the Bowie knife from the flames, its shiny blade had turned black. Thinking about Burden and the Mexicans made Logan feel plumb loco. The only thing he could do to ease it was to stab the Bowie knife deep into the ground.

Agent Granville Wulfric Dooley II had slept like a baby his first night under the stars and, at dawn, Parker had to kick his sleepy, blanket-wrapped behind to wake him. Parker remembered the motto on Dooley's card and laughed to himself. Once Dooley had yawned himself into conscious-ness and attempted a tricky wet shave on his stub-ble beard, the pair set off again towards border territory. Several times Dooley attempted to apolo-gize for the burning incident but Parker remained grim-faced and silent, hiding the fact that he was grateful to jumpy old Dooley for wiping out the most dubious chapter of his past, or rather his father's past. Parker even had difficulty now recalling the words that had been so imprinted on his memory. He smiled and allowed Dooley the relief of seeing him smile.

The gunshots that had led to this minor liberation had been closer than either man had suspected. As Parker and Dooley journeyed on through the dry scrubland, they stumbled upon evidence of the fight: the scattered possessions of a settler family; a few feathered Indian arrows laid out on the ground or stuck into it like strange flowers. There were, Parker noticed, numerous tracks from unshod horses, plus the twin channels made by a wagon's wheels. Parker halted his horse and reached down into the saddle-bag pouch by his left leg, removing a small brass field telescope. Tugging his reins, Dooley turned back to Parker as he extended the eyeglass and scanned the rocky trail ahead of them. Shielding his eyes from the sun, Dooley nervously pivoted in the saddle to scour the surrounding hills too.

'Comanche?'

Parker remained silent. Through the telescope he could see a covered prairie wagon tipped over on its side, its two horses cut loose and commandeered by the Comanche raiding party. Boxes, barrels, clothing and even a majestic doll's house had been rummaged through and were now strewn around the wagon. Parker lowered the telescope and spurred his mount gently on. Dooley lingered, drawing his new revolver from the hideout holster under his arm and cocking the hammer, a sound that made Parker's trigger finger twitch instinctively. Dooley took aim at one of the many silhouetted buzzards that circled overhead, his tongue partly extended and one eye squinting.

'No target practice yet, Dooley,' said Parker without turning back. 'They could still have scouts nearby.'

Dooley thought for a second, finger tensed on the trigger, then lowered the gun and made it safe. He followed Parker towards the prairie wagon, deciding to keep his head down and act the apprentice for the next few miles.

Parker had dismounted and trodden carefully around to the underside of the wagon by the time Dooley caught up. He had found the bodies of two settlers there, a man and a woman. While Parker searched their pockets for documentation, Dooley peered through the curtained windows of the doll's house. He could see tables and chairs, a little grandfather clock and chandeliers.

'I live in a place just like this back home,' he said, forlornly. 'Only bigger.'

Parker retrieved some papers and stood up, examining them.

'Land of opportunity, my ass,' said Parker, bitterly.

Dooley held up a small doll with plaited yellow wool for hair. 'What happened to the child?'

'She'll be raised a Comanche, if her new folks have that long,' Parker said, enigmatically. He folded the papers and pocketed them so he could report the attack later, then returned to his horse. Dooley looked up, confused, still holding the doll.

'We must at least bury them,' he said, appalled.

Parker was on his horse and began to ride onwards, ignoring the protest. Dooley stood alone, holding up the doll and hating this savage land more than ever.

They came across their first pueblo north of the Rio Grande an hour later. Dooley had long since given up checking his gold pocket-watch and was just glad to get into the shade and out of the saddle. It was a small settlement of adobe huts, a few trading posts and a small church. Stray dogs probably outnumbered the people. Parker and Dooley had happened upon an annual religious festival in the pueblo and Dooley momentarily perked up as he absorbed the local colour. A procession was moving slowly down the main avenue, women scattering flower-petals on the ground; men wearing red silk sashes around their waists and carrying a plinth with a fancy statue of the Virgin Mary weeping and clasping her hands.

Dooley shook his head in awe, smiling broadly. The air was filled with the sound of a solemn hymn.

They watched for a while and for Parker it was a suggestion of things to come. Mexico was close, he could taste it like the salt spray from an ocean. As Parker had promised, they found a cantina that seemed like an oasis in the desert. Dooley drank warm *cerveza* from a wooden cup and ate a shallow helping of mouth-burning chilli from a tin plate. Parker, meanwhile, was stood in the doorway locked in conversation with a gaunt-looking Mexican. The local wore loose white trousers and tunic and a large, round sombrero, and even had a drooping moustache just like Dooley had seen in pictures published in the city. Parker returned as Dooley was eating his second plateful.

'You should go easy, detective,' warned Parker. 'Your belly isn't prepared for Mexican cooking yet.'

'I could eat a horse,' Dooley mumbled through a mouth full of chilli.

'You are. We can't stay here much longer,' said Parker. 'Got to cover more territory.'

'But I thought we'd stay here the night?' Dooley whined, hopeful for a slice of cherry-pie or whatever passed as pudding in these parts.

Parker gestured to the gaunt Mexican.

'The old man's a buddy of mine,' he said. 'He says four Americans have been tracking us all the way from Terlingua.'

'Regulators?' asked Dooley, suddenly serious.

'But not the full deck,' said Parker. 'Which makes me nervous about what the stragglers are doing back in town.'

Dooley shook his head and scraped the last spoonful of chilli into his mouth. Parker explained how he had instructed the Mexican to delay the Regulators as much as possible. He had been wrong about not needing extra guns on this crossing, so he set right his bad judgement by making an offer on an old Spencer carbine the Mexican kept at home. It would be sufficient to keep their pursuers at bay.

The gaunt man's son had been instructed to water the Americans' horses and while they waited for him and for the Mexican to bring the carbine, Parker and Dooley wandered towards the little church. The procession had reached its destination there with the statue carried inside the doors and set down at the altar. Parker and Dooley stopped in the doorway and peered inside at all the gold decoration.

'We're the hunted now too, Dooley,' said Parker.

Dooley said nothing. Hearing the clip-clop of hoofs, they turned to see their horses being led by the boy to the front of the church. Parker and Dooley mounted up and moments later Parker's Mexican friend fetched him the carbine and a bandolier full of rounds, which Parker slipped over his shoulder. He then dropped a few dollar-pieces into the man's hand and squeezed his shoulder affectionately. Evidently, Dooley thought, the gaunt man was some sort of preacher as well as an arms dealer, for he offered Parker an elaborate blessing as they rode out of the pueblo on the petal-strewn road.

In fact, Parker's troubles had just got a whole lot worse. He knew for sure now that his enemy Bloody Bill had divided his men, and that meant the Hernandez family was his objective. The lever-action carbine Parker had bought from the Mexican felt fine in his hands. It was a .52 calibre repeater issued to cavalrymen and could be fired comfortably and quickly from the saddle. He contemplated laying an ambush for the four trackers, taking care to leave one alive for interrogation. No, Parker thought. They were outnumbered badly enough and would instead wait until the Rio Grande, perhaps try to lose the Regulators in the mountain terrain around the snaking river. Still one uncertainty persisted in Parker's mind: was Bill Logan among the four?

Unlike Parker, the gaunt Mexican wouldn't have known Bloody Bill Logan from Wild Bill Hickok. All the same, he nervously watched the more wicked of the Bills lead the Regulators into his pueblo. They arrived two hours after Parker and Dooley had departed, enough for a good headstart and for their dust cloud to settle, the Mexican thought. Just as Parker had instructed, he promptly set about tempting the party to linger a while.

'Welcome, *señor*, sit down, have drink!' the gaunt man prattled nervously.

A bottle of tequila was produced and the serving-girl behind the bar smiled seductively on cue. Logan's three men – Gray, Mulligan and Avery – were sold instantly, taking seats and chugging back the liquor so heartily the gusano worm in the bottle almost got swallowed too. But Logan himself sensed the jittery atmosphere and read the Mexican's welcome as fake. He was characteristically quick to turn violent. Logan struck the man's jaw with his quirt whip, yelling in broken Spanish how stalling was a bad idea. As he moved in closer and drew his revolver, the *señorita* stopped smiling and started to scream. She blurted out all that had gone on two hours before: the hungry gringo, the scheming Ranger, the expensive carbine. She started screaming again when Logan put a bullet in the two-faced Mexican and casually walked back outside.

'Sober up, you damned jug-heads,' Logan bawled to his men as they followed him out. 'You'll land in shallow graves come Sunday, every damned one of you.'

'Where we headed, Bloody Bill,' asked Avery with a southern drawl, looking up at the chief with admiration.

'El Carricito, you dumb bastard.'

'The stakes just got raised, huh, Parker?' said

Dooley. 'I reckon I'd better listen to what you say from here on.'

'It'll be likewise if I ever get to visit you in New York City,' replied Parker knowing well he would never set foot in the metropolis.

'Wouldn't that be something?' pondered Dooley, smiling. 'Plenty of crimes in a big city to get your teeth into.'

'Oh, there are enough right here,' said Parker. 'And they're a little more savage than your city crimes,' he added.

'You'd be surprised, partner.'

They rode on that way for a couple of hours, talking about how odd Parker would look in Little Italy or the Bronx. When the ground got treacherously uneven and the light began to fade, Parker suggested they set up camp for the night. There was precious little cover in the barren stretch of terrain they found themselves in, the best they could do was to start a fire and huddle in their Navajo blankets until dawn.

Parker didn't sleep at all and was sure the blanket-draped mound that was Dooley hadn't either. He had the unsettling feeling of being watched from the dark, probably by a coyote, Parker reasoned. Or were the Regulators closing in? After a few sleepless hours, Parker had relaxed into a semi-dream that filled his mind with disjointed thoughts. He pictured himself in Terlingua the day Angel and his rebels rode in, recreating a mental scene based on the boy's description. Of course, in this version, Parker was there to save Rose Morrison *before* the mystery bullet hit her. Drawing his six-shooter, Parker pulled Rose aside and returned fire. When he did so, the face of his enemy was masked.

SIX

As light filtered into the night sky, Parker was thankful for the new day. Dooley must have dozed off at some point as he now lay on his side, still wrapped in the thick blanket. Parker unfurled his own covering and stood up, stretching his aching body and folding the blanket away. When Dooley woke it was with the violent jerk of an interrupted dream. Parker saw that his face was pale and tired.

'Sleep well, Dooley?' asked Parker.

'I thought *you* were a nightmare and that I'd wake up in a soft bed back East,' he complained, rubbing his eyes.

Parker laughed. 'Fitful, huh?'

By the time the morning light had really arrived, they were back on the trail. Dooley had trouble staying awake in the saddle, but lack of sleep made Parker feel extra alert. As they cut through the bed of a dry stream with rocky outcrops rising up either side of them, Parker spotted the tip of a bow moving from behind a boulder. He knew instantly it was the Comanche raiding party.

'When I move you follow me *fast*, understand, Dooley?' he whispered.

'What's going on?' asked Dooley nervously.

Parker did not answer. Instead he spurred his horse's ribs sharply.

'*Yah!*' he bellowed, charging off down the dry path.

Despite the forewarning, Dooley was taken by surprise and had to ride into Parker's mushrooming cloud of dust. As he thundered along, Dooley could see movement on the overlooking rocks now. There were, he guessed, perhaps five braves, all painted for battle. He spurred his own horse on faster. As deadly arrows began cutting down into the valley floor, Parker's plan was to outrun the Comanche into open land, then turn and retaliate with the two rifles. He hoped Dooley had bothered to unwrap and load his Winchester. Parker had been troubled by Indian raiders on previous occasions and knew there was a strategy for surviving their fierce attacks.

With the two dead settlers in mind, Dooley wasn't going to wait for flat terrain to start firing, though. He pulled out the untested Remington revolver and began firing haphazardly up at the rocky battlements. The shots boomed out and Dooley felt he was getting the hang of a cavalry charge. Except that this was actually a retreat.

Perhaps the kick of the revolver, its noise, or even his lack of concentration unbalanced him, as he tumbled from the saddle and landed heavily in a scrub bush. The impact stunned him for a moment, his vision blanked out and his mind was unable to make coherent thoughts.

Parker and both horses continued racing ahead, leaving Dooley bruised and alone with the Comanche. He got to his feet and shook his dazed head, then aimed the revolver at arm's length and waited for the thick cloud of dust to settle. The fall had broken the lens in the right eye of his spectacles, so that the glass there was like a spider's web and hard to see through. The first Parker knew of Dooley's fall was when the empty-saddled horse overtook him. Parker immediately yanked on the reins of his steed and turned on a penny back into the valley. But the Comanche were already descending upon Dooley.

The detective fired and killed one brave as he scaled down the slope, then wounded another who was taking aim from the peak. Dooley had counted his shots and knew he had only one bean left in the wheel. Foolishly, he thought, he had left his ammunition in the saddle-bags – a gunbelt might have been more suitable than a shoulder rig after all. The overriding image in his mind was of being scalped by an Indian and left to bleed. Dooley knew he would hope to keep that last round for himself.

Where's that smart-ass Parker when you need him?

Dooley thought as he looked along the parched riverbed behind him. Turning back, Dooley saw a Comanche charging headlong towards him with a tomahawk poised. The brave let out a blood-curdling Comanche yell as Dooley took aim at his shoulder and fired, spinning him out of action. Dooley approached the wounded Comanche and knelt over him. He took the little doll from his belt and held it up to the man's suffering eyes.

'Where's the little girl?' he barked, cocking the hammer on his useless revolver. Dooley shook the doll and repeated the question with more urgency.

'Where?'

The Comanche's gaze shifted over Dooley's shoulder. Dooley himself was oblivious of any approach until he heard the soft crunch of foot-steps. He froze, then the wounded Comanche used all his remaining strength to grasp Dooley's waistcoat. Dooley looked over his shoulder and saw a second Comanche tower over him, this brave armed with a rifle.

'Oh Lord,' whispered Dooley. 'This is it, Granville,' he thought, perhaps out loud, perhaps internally. He closed his eyes. The Indians might have been familiar with the distinct boom of a Spencer carbine, but poor Dooley was plain baffled when the armed brave tumbled forward on to the ground. Seeing, however, that the advantage had tipped in his favour, Dooley quickly slugged the wounded Comanche who still had hold of him, knocking him unconscious. It was only then that he saw Parker step through the smoke and dust with the old carbine over his shoulder. Parker offered Dooley a hand and helped him to his feet. They both looked around in shared amazement that the detective had almost single-handedly repelled the attack.

'You saved my life, Parker,' said Dooley as he holstered the Remington.

'It's always that one last bullet that counts, isn't it?' Parker observed.

Dooley took the reins of his horse, which Parker had led back, and drew his Winchester out from the saddle boot. He cocked the lever and followed Parker among the bodies of the dead Comanches.

'Will there be others?' asked Dooley as he crouched down and touched the black hair of one dead brave, a feather tied into its strands. They were, Dooley thought, quite stunning in their savagery. 'They fought like they were possessed by demons,' he said.

The Comanche had a reputation for evil among palefaces, but Parker was of the opinion the Comanche had been here first. Now the Shoshonean tribes were a dying breed and they knew it.

'The buffalo herds have been destroyed; the Comanche are being forced on to reservations in Indian Territory,' said Parker. 'What would you do if your life was taken away piece by piece while you were busy living it?'

Dooley looked back down to the dead warrior. With the Winchester in one hand, he wrenched off the stiff, starched collar that had come loose from his shirt and threw it to the ground.

Parker didn't like to shoot *any* man in the back. But Dooley's life had depended on it, and Parker owed him one. A milestone had been reached back there in the valley: they had both now fired their guns and taken life alongside each other. It would be that way when they crossed the Rio Grande for the showdown with Angel. But would Parker's loyalty to Don Vicente mean turning his gun on Dooley? Parker couldn't imagine it coming to that. He was sure about one thing though, the Regulators tailing them had made good time and gained plenty of ground. Using his telescope, Parker could make out the dust kicked up by their horses. Parker and Dooley would have to move fast or there would be more gunplay.

The Rio Grande del Norte otherwise known in Mexico as the Rio Bravo, got its very fitting name from the long, meandering nature of its waters, rather than its width or depth. In some parts, an experienced rider could cross on horseback without much difficulty, and it was just such a spot that Parker was looking for now. Dooley called out excitedly when he first spotted the water, like a child on a trip to the beach. They stopped at the edge of the rocky bank and for a while looked down into the valley of the fast-flowing river. Cautiously, the horses took their first steps down the shifting rock bank towards the water's edge. A few times the hoofs of each horse stumbled and slid until the animals regained their footing. Once level with the water, the riders hesitated a moment before moving into the river.

'Ready for a bath, Dooley?'

'If you're sure the bridge isn't built yet.'

They spurred their horses gently forward. Only a few feet from the edge the river had risen over the top of Parker and Dooley's boots, but at its deepest point in the centre the river turned as green as an ocean. Dooley's horse struggled, snorting and shaking its head. Its legs stumbled and Dooley knew his lack of horsemanship skills were the main reason. Parker, who had crossed the river many times before and knew well how to anticipate its currents and depth, gripped his reins tightly and called back to Dooley.

'Hard on that rein, Dooley,' he said. 'And keep them knees tight together.'

Dooley followed his instructions and the horse responded.

'I think ... I'm ... getting the hang of it,' Dooley struggled to say.

'Watch them swirls.' Parker was talking about the strong undercurrents that whirled around the thin legs of the horses. His own horse whinnied and hesitated. Dooley followed his instructions and soon they were stepping up out of the river, flanks and saddles slicked black with dripping water.

'You fought the Bravo and won,' said Parker. 'Welcome to old Mexico, Dooley.'

There was something about Mexico that felt like home for Parker. He found it romantic, dangerous, melancholy . . . *alive*. He had absorbed all the best and worst of its culture, like any good American abroad, developing a taste for the burritos and tequila, the mariachi music, and even customizing his wardrobe with touches of locally produced apparel. But south of the border had also come to symbolize death and ruthlessness, and this manhunt, more than any other, would bring that too close to home, Parker thought. For the fugitives whom Parker was charged with rounding up, Mexico was freedom – their dream of freedom at least, for Parker seldom failed to catch his quarry. It meant sanctuary and a place where the dollars from a big score could stretch for a lifetime, and a lifetime fit for a king at that; it meant fiestas and siestas; long, sultry evenings, and unholy *señoritas* with holy names. Parker knew too that it meant the last outpost before the end of the world, and that his journey could well end in the sun-baked pueblo of El Carricito. For all these reasons he loved Mexico.

*

The big man was dressed only in his faded pink long johns as he splashed creek-water on his stubbly face. The seat of Mulligan's drawers sagged down towards his knees and below the water-line he'd even kept his socks on. This was the way a fellow like Mulligan took a rare bath. He hobbled back to land to dry off by the fire, where the other three Regulators, including Logan, were drinking fresh brewed Arbuckle's coffee.

'*Jeez Louise*, that water's cold enough to freeze a buffalo's . . .'

Logan poured the dregs of his black coffee from the battered tin cup into the fire. The flames sizzled at the odd fuel. A mile back along their trail, the Regulators had found evidence of Parker and Dooley's skirmish with the Comanches. Logan's man Gray had a quarter Cheyenne blood in his veins and he was a smart tracker. He followed the two sets of shod hoof-prints patiently before slipping down from his steed and picking up Dooley's discarded collar and brass .45 bullet jackets from the ground. By providence or good fortune they'd managed to pick up the lawmen's trail and Logan could almost smell those do-good star-toters already.

'Hell, Mulligan, you look a hundred pounds lighter without all that dirt,' joked Avery.

'Hobble your lip and boil me up them grounds for some *cafecito*,' snapped Mulligan as he dripped creek-water on to the rocks and shivered.

72

Avery stepped up to the fire and swirled the grounds in the bottom of a tin jug. He slopped out the black water into a filthy cup and handed it to Mulligan.

'You figure the lawmen got jumped by feather-heads, Bill?' he asked as he slurped the coffee.

'It was a Comanche raiding party and *they* got whipped by the white men,' answered Gray.

Mulligan sucked the bitter liquid off the surface of his tongue.

'You'd know, wouldn't you, scout?' he said, resentment seething.

'We're all Regulators,' Logan intervened, 'in the employ of Mr Mulhearn's Cattlemen's Association. That's official, that means *we*'re here to rub the law officers clean out. Ain't down to the natives.'

When the tension had simmered down, Gray stamped the fire out while Avery rinsed the tinware in the creek and Mulligan put his boots and breeches on. Logan was standing, hands on hips, shaking his head at his band of idiots. *I've plumb turned into a schoolma'm like Miss Rose*, he thought as he spat his tobacco.

All except Avery heard the whoosh of air that swept through the camp in the wake of the arrow. Before anyone could get a handle on what the curious noise was, he had groaned in pain, stiffened up and grabbed his left side. The feathered arrow had stuck right in his ribs and sent him toppling face first into the creek, bloodying the water a touch. Logan was drawing his six-shooter when he heard the chilling Comanche yell from behind him. It made all the hairs on the back of his neck stand up straight and it took all his gumption to spin on his heels to face the danger. The warrior was charging at him, hanging off the saddle like only a Comanche horseman could.

'Injuns!' Logan cried.

SEVEN

They had dried off in the blistering sun by the time they came across a farmstead with smoke drifting from the chimney. The roof of the shabby cabin was dry grass and on the land all around it chickens pecked at the dirt. A middle-aged man, scrawny and carrying a big shotgun came to greet them.

'What's your business?' the man said in Spanish. Parker knew he was American from his face and the strong accent in his speech. He replied in English.

'Fine place you've got here, friend.' Parker reached into his pocket and took his Ranger star out. He tossed it down to the man. 'We're lawmen on a manhunt,' he said. 'We'd appreciate someplace to eat and rest before we move on to El Carricito.'

The man looked at the badge, then studied Dooley carefully. He surely didn't look like a bandit or outlaw. The man lowered the shotgun and handed the badge back to Parker, smiling.

'Tether your steeds in the barn yonder, the wife'll fix you boys up with some victuals and hot coffee.'

Parker smiled back. 'Much appreciated,' he said.

The horses were relieved of their heavy loads and allowed to chew away at the feed in the barn. Parker stroked the back of his horse and whispered into its ear. Funny, Dooley thought, that out here a man's beloved pet was also his chief mode of transport.

By the time Parker and Dooley crossed the threshold of the homestead cabin, the man's wife, a plump Mexican woman, had set a fine table. The guests were directed to a china bowl of water that sat with a jug and towel on a dresser in the corner of the room. They washed and dried their calloused hands, then removed their hats and stood humble as churchgoers before taking seats at the long dining-table. Parker surveyed the spread and smiled contently at the glowing fireplace that provided the heart of this home. He was half-way to reaching for a chunk of bread when he saw Dooley, head bowed and hands clasped together in prayer. Parker shrank back, embarrassed by his own lack of domestic etiquette. Inmaculada could teach him the right way to be, he thought, but she would also have found his inelegance endearing. The head of the table spoke out and banished the thought of Inmaculada smiling mischievously at Parker through candlesticks and wine glasses.

'Lord, thank you for this food and for bringing these here guests to our door.'

Parker broke with personal tradition and added his own reluctant 'Amen' with the others because, Lord or no Lord, he was truly thankful for this particular slice of hospitality. As they delved at last into their lentil stew, the homesteader could no longer contain the urge to ask about the manhunt, the main reason for his hospitality.

'You're headed for El Carricito you say?'

Parker answered through a mouthful of stew. 'Right. Do you know it?'

'It's hot as hell and half as friendly,' he warned. 'Especially to lawmen like yourselves.'

'We're not here on a social call,' added Dooley, his eyes fixed on his food.

'Our quarry is a mustang named Angel Hernandez,' said Parker. 'The boy fled south after shooting dead a schoolmistress in Terlingua.'

'Everybody flees south, don't they,' said the homesteader with a slight smile.

'Do you have any idea what a youthful fugitive might be doing in El Carricito?' asked Parker. He sipped the strong black coffee from a tin cup.

'I know what I'd be doing,' the homesteader said, cackling. A dark-eyed glance from the otherwise silent Mexican woman was enough to scold him. His smile faded and he adopted a serious tone after feigning a coughing-fit. Parker caught the look and knew instantly who the real boss was.

77

'This country isn't anyone's idea of paradise right now,' the homesteader said bitterly. 'General Ortega has been squeezing the peasant population down here for all they're worth.' He spat. 'He pretty much rules El Carricito now that he's defeated his arch rival, Vasquez.'

'We'll have to keep our wits about us then,' said Parker, directing the comment at Dooley. 'Though I can't imagine Angel allying himself to such a character. The boy was always an idealist,' he continued.

'There's some opposition,' said the homesteader, rubbing his stubble chin. 'But Ortega's one ruthless *hombre*.'

Parker soaked the last of the lentil stew off his plate with bread and sat back in his chair.

'Thank you, ma'am,' he said to the woman.

'How did you come to settle down here?' a curious Dooley asked the homesteader as he collected the empty plates.

'Like I said, we all run south,' the man replied.

They sat around the fireplace for a good few hours after dinner, listening for the most part to the homesteader's bittersweet recollections and unfulfilled dreams. He had to break off in the middle of one tall tale to throw more wood on the dying fire. All the while, his wife sat in a rocking chair and worked on an embroidery panel, occasionally looking up to shake her head or roll her eyes. Parker found it all entertaining and quite touching.

'Had a little trouble with the law myself, a decade or so back,' the man confessed. 'Nothing serious you understand,' he hastened to add.

'Don't fret, our hands are full,' said Parker, smiling. He couldn't imagine the man was guilty of anything much, but then again you never could tell.

'This was her place.' The man gestured to the woman. 'She was widowed and struggling to keep it going. I rode in and never rode out, got my boots under the bed.' They were all smiling fondly, grateful for this rare moment of normality.

'Either of you fellows married or are you lone rangers?' asked the homesteader.

Dooley was keen to speak up. 'I have a sweetheart back East,' he said, producing his gold pocket-watch from his waistcoat and flipping it open. There on the inside of the lid was a small painted portrait of a red-haired woman, plain but quite charming.

'Mary O'Donnell,' said Dooley with much affection.

He grinned proudly as the homesteader studied the portrait by the flickering light of the fire.

'Ah, those Irish eyes,' the man said. The homesteader handed the watch back and turned his attention to Parker, who shifted uncomfortably in his seat. 'And how about you, son?' he asked.

Parker hesitated for a moment before giving in.

'There's a *señorita* I know, a sweet girl,' he said. 'But first I have to put her brother in jail.'

The homesteader looked uneasy and quickly changed the subject.

When he had run out of stories he looked to his wife and read her expression. There was some kind of silent confirmation, a telepathic nod of permission they both seemed to understand. A secret language between two soul mates, Parker thought.

'This isn't a big place of course,' said the homesteader. 'But you're welcome to sleep in here or take the barn.'

Parker smiled. 'Very kind,' he said. 'We'll bed down in the barn, thank you.'

Dooley was about to speak out to say he'd actually prefer the kitchen, but instead he held his tongue.

The barn was by now enveloped in the night's blackness and, apart from the occasional snorting of a nearby horse, Dooley found his improvised straw bed surprisingly comfortable. He had wrapped himself in a blanket and taken off his boots and, like Parker, had hung his gun on an otherwise useless nail that jutted out from the wall of the barn. Dooley had forgotten to bring his derby after leaving the kitchen and now wished he had it to tip over his eyes; the stars were bright and Dooley couldn't help but count them through gaps in the barn roof. When his thoughts lost all sense and structure and at last he dozed off to sleep, Parker was still brooding over the Angel dilemma. He guessed it was close to three in the morning when he was next roused from his troubled half-sleep.

Bloody Bill hadn't seen the Comanche attack coming. That failure offended him far more than the fact that one of his men now hovered close to death with a broken arrow deep in his ribs. The trail Logan's men had followed from the pueblo and across the Rio Grande, Parker's trail, had led them here to the small homestead. Here the injured Regulator could get a woman's care, at least for the last few hours of his life. Logan knew a dead man when he saw one, even if the man himself wasn't yet wise to it. It had been that way with Parker's outlaw father. Now Logan longed to look into Parker's eyes and read *his* future, knowing that if he ever got that close, Parker would be a dead man too.

Logan stepped up on to the porch of the homestead and pulled the wounded Avery down from his horse on to the ground. Unconscious, Avery landed heavily in a cloud of trail dust and with his boot-spurs jangling. That was what woke Parker: the unmistakeable sound of a lifeless body hitting the ground. Parker lifted his head and listened, frozen like a hawk for a moment. He then got to his feet, buckled on his gunbelt and kicked Dooley awake in one fluid movement. The carbine was tucked into its saddle boot and Parker grabbed it, loading a round as he found a gap in the barn to peer through.

'Look lively, Dooley,' he whispered. 'They've found us.'

Logan had lifted the wounded man to his limp feet and now hammered on the homestead door with the butt of a breech-loading Sharps rifle. The door edged open, spilling the warm glow of candlelight out into the night. Logan and the Regulators closed in on it like moths, pushing the sleepy homesteader back inside. The Mexican woman was awake too and had wrapped a shawl over her nightgown. She spoke rapidly, angrily, in Spanish with both hands held out in protest. Ignoring her, Logan hoisted Avery on to the kitchen table, sending a religious statuette flying. He tore open the man's shirt and revealed the fatal mess in his side, the stump of an arrow shaft protruding from its bloody centre.

'Fix him up,' barked Logan.

The homesteader nodded urgently to his wife and the protest ended. She began the futile business of cleaning the man's wound. Logan took a breath for the first time since he had entered the cabin. He looked down at the other man's blood staining his clothes and cursed. Then he saw something so out of place in the cabin it almost shone. He spotted, on the dresser by the water-bowl and the now bloodied towel, Agent Dooley's spotless derby. He stormed forwards and seized the hat, holding it up to the homesteader's face with a fistful of the man's nightshirt in his other hand.

'They were here?' asked Logan.

'S–Still are, mister,' he stuttered. 'Bedding down in the b–barn yonder.'

Logan's shark eyes widened before he turned back for the door, the two remaining Regulators on his heels.

Parker had climbed a ladder in the barn up to a hayloft, and through a hatch in the front wall he could see the Regulators coming in the moonlight. Aiming the carbine down on them, Parker fired into the dust at Logan's feet and the lot scattered for cover.

'Come to bushwhack a couple of lawmen, have you, Logan?' yelled Parker as he worked the carbine's lever action.

'Let's burn him out,' shouted Mulligan after a silent pause.

'Bright idea, *paisano*,' replied Parker, 'why don't you step forward.' He took aim again.

One of the Regulators, Gray, fired towards the barn from behind a rainwater barrel. Parker ducked and the bullet tore into the wood frame of the hatch. He resumed position immediately and fired, shattering the curved wooden strips of the barrel and spilling water over the cocky Regulator.

'That'll put your flame out!' shouted Parker, triumphantly.

Dooley, meanwhile, had left the barn at the back and crept with his Winchester around to the corner nearest the homestead. He saw the home-steader and his wife peer out from the window in the cabin and, when they spotted Dooley, he gestured for them to get back. Another heavy shot rang out from the loft as Parker continued firing, but from Dooley's vantage point he could see a Regulator strike a match and set fire to an improvised torch of wood, cloth and saltwort. Mulligan waited for the flame to take hold, then stood up from the plough behind which he was sheltering and reached back to throw the torch towards Parker's barn. Dooley acted quickly, aiming the rifle without much care and firing off a discouraging shot. The Regulator hollered and dropped the flame, which fell and lit up the dust. He hit the ground a second later and rolled around before scrambling for cover, clutching a bleeding arm.

One-nil, thought Dooley. Parker almost cheered too. The Regulators were on the defensive. He began to lay down a constant barrage of fire, first with the carbine and then, when it ran dry, with his six-shooter. From ground-level, Dooley caught on to Parker's tactics and followed his lead. He used the repeating rifle to its full potential, emptying the mechanism in the direction of the Regulators in a fearsome volley. When the rifle stopped repeating, he drew the Remington without losing a second and began to squeeze off rapid shots, perhaps caught up in the excitement of all that firepower.

At the receiving end, Logan was hunkered down behind the plough watching the wounded Mulligan bleed.

'Quit your squawking,' he barked at the man, struggling to be heard over the gunfire. Out of the corner of his eye, Logan saw Gray running for his horse, tethered near the cabin. He cussed under his breath and lifted Mulligan to his feet. The Regulators were outgunned.

'Ride out, damn it,' he shouted, trying to claw back some control.

Across the yard, Logan saw the cabin door open and the homesteader's wife emerge carrying a long shotgun. She aimed the scattergun at the stars and fired a wall of buckshot, then levelled the barrel at the fleeing intruders. From their own positions, both Parker and Dooley were watching her too. The woman's furious expression was clear for all to read. In confusion, the Regulators' horses bolted and circled outside the cabin, kicking up choking dust and making it near impossible to mount up. The first man to lose his nerve was already galloping away, while Logan and the wounded Mulligan struggled to control their mounts. From the saddle, Logan fired his rifle at the cabin door, forcing the woman back for cover. He just had time to shoot a glance up at the black square of the hayloft hatch before retreating into the desert night.

Silence returned to the homestead as the four gathered in front of the cabin. Dooley picked up his hat from where Logan had dropped it, dusting of its rounded crown and poking a finger through a lucky bullet hole in its side.

'Who in hell were they?' asked the homesteader.

'Mercenaries, out to kill the same man we're after,' replied Parker.

'You might have warned us,' added the woman, still holding the shotgun.

'I should have,' said Parker, looking down at his boots. 'What did they say?'

'They brung a . . .' the homesteader's voice trailed away. He and his wife made eye contact, then looked back and forth between the cabin and Parker, slack jawed. Confused, Parker and Dooley followed the couple inside. As the woman set the shotgun down, lit an oil-lamp and turned up the flame, the darkness was illuminated by a flickering glow. There on the table lay the wounded Regulator.

'Mercy,' the bemused homesteader exclaimed, scratching his head.

Until dawn, the homesteader's wife treated Avery as best she could, cooling his brow and stemming the flow of his blood. As the sun rose, he died. None of them slept much during those tense few hours of silence between the last gunshot and the first crowing of the cockerel.

'We'll bury him on the hill,' said the homesteader. 'You fellows are the closest thing to law for miles around here.'

As the sun spread light across the dawn sky, Parker and Dooley climbed up to the high ground overlooking the homestead. Parker carried the dead Regulator over his shoulder while Dooley held the shovels. They dug a hole and buried the nameless man who, given the chance, would have killed them both.

'There but for the grace of God go I,' whispered Dooley, reminded of his skirmish with the Comanche.

Play with fire, get burned, was all Parker could think. Dooley fashioned a simple cross from two sticks and thrust it into the edge of the grave-mound before both men trudged silently back down the hill. Parker had made a point of staying at the homestead until daybreak, just to protect the couple. But Logan had not returned. Now he offered the man and his wife money and remorse before riding out with Dooley. The couple would not take the money and Parker knew the apology rang hollow too.

Few words were exchanged as they rode on towards El Carricito. It was not a hostile silence, just a private one in which both men prepared for the challenges that lay ahead. Parker saw the buzzards first. They were hovering high above a patch of land ahead. It was an ominous portent that reminded Dooley of the dead settler couple. As Parker and he rode closer to the scavengers they could see dark shapes on the ground, some moving while others were dead still. The obscene squawking of the birds grew in volume until it grated in Parker's ears. He looked down from his horse as it clip-clopped past the carrion: the bodies of five men and their guns lay around a doused camp-fire. The grounded buzzards that tore away with their razor beaks had so desecrated the corpses that Parker understood Dooley's compulsion to let off a few rounds at the winged devils.

'Been dead three or four days judging by the discoloration,' said Dooley, holding a handkerchief over his nose and trying not to gag.

Parker looked down at one of the men and saw the matted scalps hanging from his belt. It was a common ritual, not restricted to Indians.

'My God,' said Dooley in disbelief.

The last man Parker saw had his face turned sideways, cheating the buzzard of the side nearest the ground. He looked closer and felt his stomach knot. At first he thought the broad Mexican face was Angel's, then he recognized it as Cortez, one of Don Vicente's trusted ranch hands.

EIGHT

The Terlingua Gentlemen's Club had been started
by Mayor Buchanan as a hideaway in which to
drink, smoke, reminisce and generally machinate.
It was a mahogany-panelled sanctuary where deals
were done and alibis were provided. Most of the
rich Anglo ranchers in the area enjoyed member-
ship, including Theodore Mulhearn. Honest folk
like Marshal McOwen didn't have a hope of ever
getting inside. Once, the old ladies' Temperance
Society had even tried to close the club down, but
Buchanan had pulled strings to get *them* closed
down instead.

On this morning, while others were out getting
bloody on their behalf, Buchanan and Mulhearn
sat talking in leather armchairs by the fireplace.

'Parker has a bee in his bonnet over murdered
damsels,' said Buchanan. 'His sense of outrage

over Rose's death will outweigh his loyalty to Casa Hernandez.'

'And if Angel convinces the Ranger of his innocence, what then?' asked Mulhearn.

'You've sent Logan down there, haven't you?' Buchanan said. 'With respect, a rather foolish action given his track record with the Burden dynasty.'

'Logan's our most thorough option.'

Buchanan glanced over his shoulder at the other members in the club, embarrassed by Mulhearn's raw, cowboy style. Mulhearn's conspiracy to grab land across the territory was all about going further than the next man. He had hired Logan and his bounty-killer 'Regulators' (a handle Mulhearn had given them himself) to rub out the competition. That meant challenging Hispanic ranchers on their own livestock, raiding their rightful land, and waging a range war against innocent immigrants and Indians. He and the other powerful Anglos he represented in the cattlemen's association had pretty much sewn up the state, all except the ranch of Don Vicente Hernandez.

'Don't lose your nerve now, Mayor,' he warned.

'The killing never ends,' sighed Buchanan.

'Don't you want to see the bank's gold returned? Don't you want to see Angel take the rap for poor Miss Rose?'

There was a moment of peace, only broken by the low hum of background chatter, the noble tick-tock of a pendulum clock and the crackle of the log-fire.

'Your harassment of Don Vicente has gotten out of hand,' warned Buchanan. 'It needs to end.'

'That's the plan,' said Mulhearn with a crooked grin.

The deep chime of the clock made it known that breakfast was served. The two men would continue their business after bacon and eggs.

'Give me one good reason not to shoot you.' Angel's ultimatum echoed around the cavern. He hated Ortega with a passion that was overwhelming, clawing at his throat like icy water to a drowning man. Sometimes, in that violent blur of emotion, Angel worried what extremes he could be capable of. Murder in the case of Ortega himself? The general deserved it. But what about those who fed off the scraps from the tyrant's table? Angel took no pleasure in killing desperate Mexicans. He liked to think of himself as one, except he knew good from bad, didn't he? The fight with the bandits was not murder, simply survival. Angel had fired the first sneaky shot and killed the scalp-hunter. When the shooting was over, five men lay dead. His friend Cortez was among them. There had been many more bandits, swarming out from the cover of the night like bats, forcing the rebels to abandon their camp . . . and their dead.

Angel struggled to fight off his self-doubt. His

91

father had always taught him that mercy was a man's finest quality; it was what made him different from an animal. But there were many men in this land without mercy who made life cheap, animals like Ortega for instance, and Angel felt no compassion for them, pale-skinned or dark. These were important issues for a leader to consider, Angel realized, as he held the six-shooter to the man's head.

'P–*Por favor*, Tauro,' the man stuttered, his face bloodless and his eyes wide with fear. 'Let me join you, I'll kill that bully Ortega.' He still wore the ragged uniform and had been captured by Angel's band during a skirmish in nearby La Jarita. After arriving in El Carricito, Angel and any Mexican willing to take up a gun with him had sought cover in this mountain hideout. Now their prisoner cowered there with his hands on his head while Angel looked down at him and tried to summon some mercy.

'If I let you live, so that you might fight with us,' suggested Angel, toying with the man, 'a treacherous pig like yourself might then betray us in thanks. As a spy, no?'

'No *señor*, you are wrong,' the prisoner replied, unnerved by the cold barrel against his sweaty forehead. 'That is to say, uh . . . I am not treach—'

'But you *are* a pig?' Angel joked, the guerrillas around him breaking into laughter. The prisoner sank down an inch, accepting his fate. '*Sí*, Tauro,' he whispered. Angel thought for a moment, then smiled and lowered the revolver.

'Then you will fit in perfectly with these desperadoes,' he said. The man looked up at Angel, bemused. 'Just lose that accursed uniform at once,' added Angel. Muttering thanks, the man was ushered away into the caverns beyond as Angel holstered his revolver. He felt like a real leader. Don Vicente had been right: it was mercy that made a man.

El Carricito was a dusty but expanding pueblo that had become a magnet for villains clean out of time and good fortune. It had always been fundamentally lawless and, most mornings, early risers would awake to find a corpse in the street, known locally as a 'dead man for breakfast'. That had been the norm even under the rule of the late *presidente* of El Carricito, Governor Pablo Vasquez – a benevolent native with a hopeless desire to clean up his town. In a move that would have impressed Mulhearn, 'General' Ortega had forced Vasquez out of office – not by means of a voting ballot but by a musket ball in cold-blooded murder. The town had become the garrison to a band of convicted thieves and murderers, pardoned from jail by Ortega. The uniforms of these *rurales* were filthy and ragged, and they now waged war through drunken banquets and taxation bordering on theft.

Parker and Dooley stopped some distance away to survey the town. They exchanged a look. In the distance, a church bell was ringing out like the echo of a dream.

'That's it, Parker,' said Dooley. 'The kid's in there somewhere.'

'Yep,' replied Parker. 'And a whole lot of trouble to boot.'

There was nothing else to do now but push forward on the last stage of their journey, so Parker and Dooley rode hard towards the gates of El Carricito.

An uncharacteristic stillness had settled over the town. The sun was hot and the air stifling, the siesta hour coming early. As Parker and Dooley rode single file down a trail behind the main street, they passed fleapit cantinas and hotels. Mule-droppings peppered the street and goats, dogs and chickens wandered freely. The church bells were still ringing; a euphoric sound which Parker guessed was in celebration of a wedding rather than a funeral.

They rode out into a dusty town plaza where the noise grew to an ugly iron din. The Mission San Juan, a crumbling, whitewashed adobe church, stood besieged at the spoiled heart of El Carricito. It was now clear why the town had seemed so still: the plaza was full of people gathered to greet the newly-weds. Parker noted that many of the men wore khaki uniforms. They paused at the edge of the crowd to watch the bride and groom emerge from the huge double doors of the church, Parker's horse swaying nervously as cheers threatened to drown out the joyful church bells. A shower of rice thrown from the crowd rained down over the bride's white lace dress, catching in her long black hair. Parker broke out of his daydream, the slight smile fading from his face. He thumped Dooley's arm to get his attention, then rode off behind the spectators.

Parker and Dooley killed some time watering their horses from a trough, splashing the same water on the backs of their sunburned necks to cool down. Parker loved the climate down here, but Dooley was finding it hard going. They were sipping watery *cerveza* and eating enchiladas in a shaded cantina when the sound of the wedding fiesta drifted in. Mariachi music and Catherine-wheel fireworks filled the plaza, which was even busier now than before. Parker and Dooley strolled outside and into the heaving crowd, the Easterner smiling and looking around him like an expectant child. The fiesta would last long into the night, indeed through to the next morning. Already a woman wearing a long red dress and with a red flower in her hair danced flamenco on a table to Parker's left. To the beat of her heels on the wooden surface, Parker scanned the crowd as revellers nudged past him. *Would Angel's face be among them,* he wondered. Dooley was cheerfully clapping his hands, the derby tilted back on his head. A laughing young girl hurried past and handed Dooley a flower, which he accepted glee-fully.

Parker noticed the faces of two Americans first, standing out just as he and Dooley no doubt did, amid the congregation of Mexicans. It took a moment to recognize them as the Regulators from the homestead stand-off, for they had both ditched their trademark dusters. One of them, however, had the bandaged arm wound of Dooley's arsonist. The men were standing guard, scanning the crowd eagle-eyed like Parker. Beyond Mulligan and Gray, Parker saw a short, pudgy Mexican wearing a fancy uniform laden with gold buttons, braid and epaulettes, who he guessed was General Ortega. The general reminded Parker of a bullfrog with mutton-chop whiskers. He was listening intently to a third American standing at his side and demon-strating the workings of a rifle. It was Logan and his Sharps.

Parker had suspected Logan would proposition Ortega about their common enemy, Angel, which in turn meant Ortega's men would now be after Parker too. Parker watched them for a while across the sea of bobbing heads. He supposed that Logan had ridden on to El Carricito after that humiliat-ing retreat. Logan would still be seething and the memory alone would drive him on to see Parker dead. This town had the explosive mixture of a powder keg and could go off at any time, Parker thought. He turned to Dooley.

'Let's rent a cheap room to lie low,' he told the

grinning detective.

'You mean an actual *room?*'

They struggled against the crowd in the opposite direction before heading off down a side-street decorated with paper lanterns. From balconies above them, soiled doves cooed down from bordellos, making Dooley blush. Parker found a suitable ground-level room in a boarding-house and dropped a silver coin into the hand of the owner in exchange for a heavy iron key.

'*Gracias,* gringos,' the owner said from the doorway as they entered the squalid room.

The four adobe walls they stood within weren't fit for habitation, but it would allow them to keep out of sight until a plan was formulated in Parker's brain.

'Your taste in lodgings never ceases to underwhelm me, Parker,' said Dooley as he eyed a cockroach on the wall.

As darkness fell over the fiesta, Parker instructed Dooley to get some shut-eye. He needed a lead on the fugitive Angel and decided the best place to start would be the priest at the Mission San Juan. He, more than anyone in El Carricito, would be wise to even the most guarded of secrets. Dooley would normally have insisted on being in on every step of the investigation, but at this stage in the journey he was too tired to care. When Parker left the room, Dooley cat-napped with the Remington in his hand.

Parker made his way through the crowd and slipped inside the church He stood before the majestic golden altar shrine as the heavy door swung slowly shut behind him and blocked out the sound of the festivities. Walking down the aisle past simple wooden pews towards the altar, the jingle bobs on his spurs chinked with each step. The priest, Father Perez, was near the sacristy, tidying away the paraphernalia of the earlier wedding ceremony. The priest turned to look at Parker, who saw that the Mexican was in his forties, with the weather-beaten face of a cowboy.

'You are welcome in the House of God, but your gun isn't,' he said.

Parker took out his Ranger star and held it up for the priest.

'Is that supposed to count for anything down here, Ranger?' The priest shrugged.

'It's a character reference cast in tin,' replied Parker. 'It applies either side of the border.'

Father Perez smiled and gestured Parker to take a seat in a pew, then sat opposite him.

'What can I do for you?' he asked.

'It's a busy day in town,' said Parker.

'The wedding of General Ortega's beloved niece,' said Perez. 'He declared an official day of celebration and threatened everyone with death unless they grinned like monkeys.'

'Ortega, huh? Need I ask your opinion of him, as a man of the Church, I mean?'

'As a man of the Church, I did not perform the correct vows – his niece's marriage will not be recognized in the eyes of God,' whispered Perez with a sly smile. 'They will be living in sin.'

Parker raised an eyebrow. 'I'm tracking Angel Hernandez,' he said. 'He's the son of my good friend, Don Vicente out of southern Texas.'

'You've come to arrest the son of a friend? Such a dilemma,' said Perez playfully.

'He killed a woman,' came Parker's terse reply.

The priest nodded.

'Angel came to me for confession, so what he said I cannot repeat,' Perez told Parker. 'But while only God knows the truth, I can say that I do not believe Angel is the killer of this woman. And neither does Angel himself.'

'When was this confession heard?' asked Parker.

'A week ago,' replied Perez. 'Not long after he rode into town.'

'His conscience must have been bothering him,' said Parker. 'Did he tell you about the robbery too, Padre?'

'Come now, Ranger. What would an old altar boy like Angel do with all that gringo gold?' the priest replied, smiling.

Parker was thoughtful for a moment, looking towards the altar shrine's crucifix. His eyes darted back to Father Perez.

'Another American is after Angel,' said Parker. 'He's a bounty hunter and he'll kill Angel when he finds him.'

Perez frowned.

'This *hombre* is called Logan and he's in El Carricito with two henchmen,' continued Parker. 'I have to hear Angel's version of events before Logan finds him, Padre.'

NINE

When Parker walked out into the night, the fiesta was still going strong. At the boarding-room, he found Dooley awake and sitting in a little wooden chair by the window. He was swaying slightly to a broken-hearted guitar ballad that drifted in on the warm night air.

'Too hot to sleep,' complained Dooley, reholstering the Remington which still lay in his lap.

Parker had worked out a plan: he would first try to find Angel; if he met a dead end Parker would go straight to the general himself. Unpleasant as that seemed, there was no time for a cat-and-mouse game down here. Don Vicente was a sitting duck out at the ranch and Logan was out there too, itching to put a bullet in Parker's back.

The priest had tipped Parker off to a house in the southern end of town, its roughest *barrio*, where Angel had apparently been hiding out. He told Parker that Angel had moved on, but to where he did not know. For Parker, Father Perez didn't quite add up.

He dragged Dooley back outside and together they walked through the darkest alleys to the unremarkable adobe hut. Parker's shooting-hand twitched near his Colt Frontier during the whole journey; this was a dangerous place, but for a pair of obvious peace officers there was, in Dooley's turn of phrase, the probability of peril.

Turning a corner in the cobbled alley, Parker saw the adobe hut they were looking for. A goat was tethered outside and a ceramic-tile panel to the side of the entrance carried the painted word *Tauro*, the second sign of the zodiac, just as Father Perez had said it would. Parker checked Dooley's readiness with a nod of the head, before drawing the revolver. The click of its hammer was the only sound in the night-time silence as they stepped in closer. Dooley followed suit, drawing the heavy Remington revolver from under his jacket, the silence too deafening to dare cock the hammer now. Parker's fingers felt for the rope hoop that served as a doorhandle. With a gentle nudge from his shoulder the rickety door began to creak open, swinging inwards on its rusted hinges over a threshold of cracked tiles.

Parker led the way inside the hut, the revolver now held out at arm's length. At that distance, without the blue glow of moonlight, Parker could not even see the gun in his own hand. He stepped blindly forward, guided only by the muffled sound of snoring which Parker's heightened hearing could detect low down from the corner of the room.

The muzzle of the Frontier made contact with some invisible surface, soft enough to give way a little to the oncoming barrel. It interrupted the drone of snoring, which was replaced by the louder muttering of a deep sleeper roused from a dream. Parker withdrew the revolver a fraction, panning it up the bed towards the source of the breathing. The muzzle closed in again until it touched the temple of a man's head on the pillow.

'Angel,' whispered Parker.

'Huh?' came the confused reply, more exhaled air than spoken word. The sleeper rose further into consciousness.

'Angel,' repeated Parker, this time louder.

The sound of breathing had ceased. Parker heard the creak of a straw mattress and saw the wet glint of a staring eye before the shouting started. The barrage of Spanish was so loud and locally accented that Parker couldn't understand a word the man was saying. The basic message was clear even to Dooley though. After a few seconds, Parker swung the revolver down through the darkness and made contact. The screams fell silent. Dooley stepped forward with a matchbox and struck a flame that fizzed to life and cast an orange ball of light on to his own worried face. Dooley held the flame between his hands, hovering closer towards the bed and settling the glow on to the once more unconscious man. Parker saw right away that it was not Angel.

'He looks older, no?' said Dooley.

The match flame died out and darkness filled the room again.

'Damn it,' Parker whispered in the shadows.

The shouting had woken a stray dog, now barking furiously from somewhere further up the alleyway. Several shuffling footsteps were running towards the adobe hut too. Parker spun around to the door and saw the figures silhouetted in its arch. This time he understood the Mexican chatter enough to know they were Ortega's men.

Parker was relieved he hadn't killed the man in his own bed. It didn't matter much to the unkempt soldiers as they dragged Parker and Dooley outside, but the man mistaken for Angel slowly began to wake for the second time.

'Where are they taking us, Parker?' asked Dooley as he was manhandled along.

'An audience with General Ortega,' replied Parker, translating the conversation. 'I'll do the talking,' he added.

Like all the best megalomaniacs, Cesar Ortega was on the short side. To compensate, he wore a pair of Cuban-heeled leather riding-boots that went up to his fat thighs and needed two helpers to pull off of a night. Along with the rest of his Napoleonic duds the man looked exactly like what he was: a relic of the past. Somehow he had seized this time and place as his own, but his empire was a sham and would soon crumble. He held court in an old wine cellar and was steadily drinking its remaining stock dry. There was an ornamental throne, looted from Vasquez's study, set against one mouldy wall and an oil-portrait of Vasquez was propped against it. Ortega had slashed at the canvas with a sword. Banquet tables were arranged before the throne, loaded with food and *vino* for his army of thugs. A few chickens, tomorrow's dinner, pecked around the floor, while blank-faced women and children sat around idly, some dressed in oversized army cast-offs. This inner circle was idle, growing fat and enjoying the illusion of living on the plush while it lasted. They would kill just about anyone to protect their lot.

Ortega was seated on his throne with his niece, in the finery of her wedding dress, perched on his knee when Parker and Dooley were brought before him. He was puffing away on one of the fine cigars also looted from Vasquez. Parker listened to a guard's explanation, which was some nonsense about robbers and assassins. He wondered for a moment whether Father Perez would really have stooped to informing for Ortega's regime. Dooley kept his eyes on the ground while Parker stepped forward. Both men had been relieved of their side-arms.

'General Ortega,' said Parker, removing his Stetson and bowing his head without a grain of true sincerity. 'And the lovely bride. Congratulations, *señorita.*'

'Who is this gringo?' Ortega asked one of the soldiers, voice slurred from too much drink. Parker decided to play it bold. He casually reached into his pocket and retrieved the tin star. The soldiers around him tensed, a dozen muskets aimed his way. Parker pinned the badge on his lapel and straightened up proudly. Dooley looked nervous but remembered Parker's warning to keep quiet. A booming American voice called out from the corner of the cellar.

'It's Parker Burden, Texas Ranger, that's who.'

Parker turned his head and found Logan stepping towards him, the two Regulators Gray and Mulligan in his shadow. His jaw clenched in anticipation of a fight.

'Ah hah!' Ortega enthused, his eyes widening in delight.

'I'll take him outside and shoot him for you, General.' Logan pronounced the word '*Hen-er-al*,' as he hurriedly drew his six-shooter.

Parker faced off to him, speaking urgently in English. 'Kill us and Angel will hunt you down.' He turned to Ortega, 'All of you.'

'What is this you say?' asked Ortega in pidgin English, craning his neck forward.

'Angel and he is good buddies,' added Logan.

Ortega pushed the girl from his knee and stood.

'Don Vicente Hernandez is my friend,' announced Parker. 'I'm here to apprehend his son, a bank-robber.'

'And killer,' added Logan.

106

'Apprehend?' repeated Ortega.

'Where is he, Burden?' asked Logan, grinning. He lowered his voice to a whisper and leaned towards Parker, 'Tell me and we'll split the gold.'

'He's here in El Carricito, no?' Parker continued. 'This man . . .' Parker was gesturing to Logan when the bounty hunter spun his six-shooter around on one finger by the trigger guard and cracked the wooden grip against Parker's jaw. Dooley stepped towards him and Logan spun the revolver again to aim at the detective. Parker slumped to the floor and landed on his hands and knees, spitting blood and shaking the stars out of his eyes.

Parker's head was lolling and syrupy blood was hanging in a cord from his jaw. The cobbled floor in front of his eyes was awash with dark red liquid, so his first panicked thought was of haemorrhaging. When the scent of wine filled his nostrils, Parker knew he was chained up among the vats.

'Parker, you all right?' came Dooley's voice. The detective was chained alongside him. Parker spat and looked at the iron cuffs that bound each man's wrists, keeping them down on the cold cobbles with their backs to a huge distillery barrel.

'What do we do, Parker?'

Footsteps on the wet stone floor echoed to their left. Parker's eyes focussed on Logan's heavy silhouette coming their way.

The *click* of six-shooter metal being cocked. . . .

Parker swallowed deeply and tasted the rusty tang of blood. He felt a jagged, broken tooth with his tongue.

'Seems history is repeating, Burden,' said Logan's silhouette. He stepped into a shaft of moonlight from some small window to the outside world, part of his bearded face suddenly glowing silver.

Parker nodded. 'Seven years on and you're still springing ambushes to make a kill,' he replied.

Logan knelt in the wine puddle by Parker's side and tapped the revolver against his tin Ranger's star.

'Nah, I'll let you know when the bullet's a-comin',' he sneered. Logan moved the six-shooter up to Parker's bloody mouth and pushed the barrel against his teeth. It made the same little clinking noise as the badge.

'*And it's a-comin' soon.*'

Father Perez had got word of the two American lawmen imprisoned by Ortega. He stormed into the cellar and, in his own unconventional manner, talked Ortega round with a volley of rapid-fire Spanish. The Ranger, he claimed, was here to officially arrest Angel Hernandez for the murder of a young white woman. Angel would not escape the noose. What better way to discredit his enemy and quash the rebellion? Ortega thought about it through his mescal haze for a moment, then with a sweep of his hand he summoned his soldiers. The Mexicans flooded into the vat chamber like a sonora and interrupted Bloody Bill at his work.

'Release these men at once,' the priest demanded. 'That is an order. *Andale*.'

'Hang on a goddamn minute, sin doctor,' Logan protested.

'An order from General Ortega himself.'

Father Perez nodded knowingly to Parker. The chains were released and Parker and Dooley were led away by the priest. Cheated, Logan stayed put and watched them go, six-shooter still in hand. When all was quiet, he would put a bullet into one of the vats and watch the fountain of red liquid spurt out, imagining he had just shot Parker. As the lawmen made their exit, Ortega stepped forward and looked up at six-footer Parker.

'Angel Hernandez is a bad kid,' he said. 'I too would like very much to see him "apprehended".'

'What did you do to become his enemy, General?' Parker spoke through his bleeding lips.

Ortega laughed through his nose. 'He's a *guerrillero*, his gang lives in the hills and comes down only to rob and kill.'

'A bad kid,' said Parker.

The steps up from Ortega's wine vault led straight on to the plaza of the Mission San Juan. Parker and Dooley holstered their side-arms and were escorted out to street level by Perez. Parker removed the tin star from his jacket front and put it in his pocket. He hated doing so as it made him feel like an unsanctioned mercenary. Irritated, Parker watched as the last fiesta *mariachi* band moseyed from the plaza, guitar over shoulder.

'Much appreciated, Padre,' said Parker. 'If you don't mind, we won't linger.'

'You should have trusted a priest,' said Perez. 'Poor Paco woke with a mean headache.'

'He's lucky I didn't shoot him,' replied Parker impatiently.

'Ortega's men are everywhere,' said Perez. 'You must learn to be more like the rattlesnake than the bison.'

'Does Angel know that while we're playing cloak-and-dagger games, his father's ranch is in danger?'

Father Perez shrugged fatalistically.

From the far end of the plaza, across its littered and dusty floor, a young boy came running towards them. He was seven or eight years old, with coal-black hair and dirty white peasant clothes. When he reached them he was out of breath and excited.

'Mister Ranger,' he said in broken English. 'Tauro sends for you.'

TEN

The boy called Chico led Parker and Dooley on a magic-hour tour to the local bull-ring for the meeting with Tauro. That was what the locals had called Angel, the boy explained, ever since he had hidden in the house of the same name. Now though, Tauro had disappeared into the hills. Parker at least felt comforted that the priest had been genuine after all.

The bull-fighting ring was a wooden stadium with a sand arena stained with old blood. Chico led the Americans half-way down the enclosure leading to the ring, then put two fingers to his mouth and let out a shrill whistle. He promptly turned on his heels and raced off in the direction they had all just come from, without further explanation. Parker and Dooley were left alone in the silence.

'Angel?' Parker said hesitantly, pronouncing the

name *Ankel* like a native. The call echoed along the tunnel.

They walked slowly towards the first light that had begun to fill the ring in the moments before dawn.

'Be sure to slug the right guy this time, please,' whispered Dooley. Three or four steps closer and the figure of a large man sidestepped into their path.

'Parker Burden?' the man drawled in a thick accent.

'Where's Angel? Where is Tauro?' asked Parker.

They continued to within a few feet of the large man. Parker saw his pock-marked face and black beard.

'I am Tauro,' said the man.

Parker thought for a moment then laughed.

'You're too old and too ugly,' he said. 'Did Angel send for me or not?'

He continued up to the big man and stared him down. For a few tense seconds it seemed either man might reach for his shooting-iron.

'Let him pass,' said an unknown voice from inside the bull-ring.

The impostor breathed a sigh of relief and stood aside. Parker slipped past him, Dooley following. Parker saw half a dozen other Mexican rebels gathered around the perimeter of the ring, all ghost shadows in the night. Parker circled in the dust, studying the shadowy faces around him. Only one was familiar. The man swaggered towards him, wearing a sombrero, smiling.

'Paco,' said Parker, surprised. 'How's the head?'

'How do I know if we can trust you?' he asked. 'Or the Yankee there.' The sleeping rebel gestured to Dooley, who suddenly looked awfully self-conscious.

'Agent Dooley is charged with recovering stolen gold, that's all,' said Parker.

'Quite,' replied Paco without hesitation. 'Where are your horses stabled?'

'Across town,' Parker said. 'Is Angel waiting?'

Parker and Dooley were instructed to collect their horses and meet the Mexicans in the plaza. When they arrived some forty-five minutes later, the square was empty.

'What do you make of all this, Parker?' Dooley asked as they waited. Parker took a deep breath of the cool air and looked up at the bats, which still circled overhead.

'These people have elevated Angel to some kind of rebel hero,' he said. 'I have no intention of harming Angel, but he still has Rose Morrison to answer for.'

'At least our Mexican entourage will keep Logan at bay,' said Dooley.

They did not have long to wait before Father Perez emerged from the shadows on horseback, the clip-clop of hoofs drifting before him. Parker was surprised to see that he wore the simple clothes of a peasant, but with an incongruous bullet bandolier slung over his shoulder. Following closely behind were the other ghosts of the bull-ring, including Paco.

Parker said nothing about the mystery priest, deciding to keep quiet and play things by ear. Silently they rode out along the back-street trail towards El Carricito's gates. As the expanse of desert appeared beyond the pueblo buildings on the outskirts of town, Dooley realized he was running on pure adrenaline. Recent events had put him way out of his depth, while the unbro-ken transition from night to day gave it all a dreamlike unreality. He shivered in the chill wind and let his mind toy with fantasies of life back East. Parker rode ahead of Dooley, scan-ning the dawn horizon for Ortega's men. His exhausted mind fixated on the assignment and its many hurdles. He was trying to find the right words to confront Angel with when the silent convoy was discovered. As Parker had feared, several of Ortega's foot-soldiers spotted the departing band of guerrillas. They ran forward with muskets poised, fumbling in belt pouches or bandoliers. Horses whinnied and bolted as their riders fired a volley of shots; there was the sudden crack of black powder, billowing smoke clouds and the lick of orange muzzle-flash. Parker and Dooley had neither the time to draw their weapons nor to check if Ortega's troops had fallen. Their element of surprise lost, the riders cried '*Vamos!*' and stampeded out of El

Carricito and across the endless sandy sea beyond. It was a burst of energy that shook Dooley awake better than a pailful of six-shooter coffee. He held on to his hat with one hand and felt the flesh on his jowls bouncing as the appaloosa gave its all. It was just like Custer's Seventh at Little Bighorn, he fancied, a glorious bugle-call sounding in his imagination.

The cavalry charge was short-lived. Without fear of pursuit, the point rider slowed to a trot with his arm held up as a signal. The dust cloud behind the convoy began to settle as the rest followed his lead. The desert was unnaturally quiet when it ended, the calm settling like a snowfall. Dooley was grinning. Parker stole a brief look back over his shoulder, past Dooley and other guerrillas, to the distant town as it was lit by the sunrise.

The journey continued without conversation or incident. Parker and Dooley followed loyally without any clue as to where the trail would end. Every so often, Parker would see the bandit priest Father Perez look back at him and flash a devious grin. Only in Mexico, Parker thought, could a preacher lead wedding vows by day and armed rebellion by night. He noticed the horses in front veer to the left, towards the rocky hills that overshadowed El Carricito. This, the boy had said, was Angel's new home.

Soon, the trail was winding up into the high ground; past caverns and outcrops, towards the carved ancient dwellings of early native Indians. As the party neared the caves, Dooley was amazed by the intricacy of their construction and how, in the new sun, they radiated a fiery orange glow. Parker's eyes were assessing the more modern signs of life that had appeared to greet them, a small gathering of peasant men, women and children. Angel's flock swarmed down to meet the horses, shaking the hands of the Mexican riders, giving Parker and Dooley only apprehensive looks.

The riders dismounted and their horses were swiftly led away into the trees beyond the trail, while the men made the short climb up a narrow path to the cave dwellings. Parker stepped inside the shade of the largest cavern doorway. The other riders were being served strong coffee and began retelling the previous night's escapades. Father Perez approached Parker and Dooley and pointed deep inside the cave. Just like one of Parker's looking-glass dreams, out of the darkness stepped Angel Hernandez.

Parker hadn't known what to expect from Angel, so much had changed in the year since their last meeting. That much was clear the second he stepped into the light in his new incarnation, Tauro. Angel had grown into a man, even aged before his time. The face was rough and tanned, and he wore a scraggy beard. The sparkle in the eyes was the same, though, as Angel came towards

Parker with open arms and a warm smile.

'Parker!' said Angel, embracing him. 'It is truly good to see you again, *compadre*, no matter the state of affairs.'

Some of the Mexican riders stopped to watch the scene, surprised by the warm reception.

'You know why I'm here?' asked Parker, sternly.

'And why Mr Dooley has travelled so far to meet me,' replied Angel. 'Come, you have yet to hear the *true* story.'

Angel led Parker and Dooley further into the cavern to a small corner of the cave network. His sleeping area was a natural hollow in the rock, surrounded by stalactites and some four feet off the level of the cave floor. Angel climbed up and held out his hand to hoist up the others. Candlelight flickered around the hollow and Dooley now saw how homely it all was: a bedroll, box table, writing-materials. He reached for a dog-eared dime novel which lay on the floor of the cave room, its cover illustration showing a cowboy hero called 'Swingdingle Sam' saving a damsel from an Indian savage.

'You like adventures?' asked Angel.

'I think I've had my fill lately,' replied Dooley as he set the book down again.

Parker had noticed a tintype photograph of the Hernandez family, propped on the box table. His gaze found Inmaculada in the assembly and remained fixed until Angel spoke.

'You have seen how this dog Ortega has bled my

people dry,' said Angel, bitterly. 'My heart is heavy when I see such injustice in El Carricito.'

'My heart is heavy too, over another injustice,' answered Parker.

'Before my father, your friend, became wealthy over the border, he was a poor man just like them,' Angel said with growing urgency. 'He too was born in El Carricito.'

'I understand why you stole the gold,' said Parker. 'To fund a rebellion or to give to the poor.'

'And you call this *in*justice?' asked Angel.

'You can't rewrite the law, not in America,' said Dooley.

'If you want to take back the gold, Mr Dooley,' said Angel, 'be my guest.'

Angel reached back to a small strongbox in the hollow and lifted back the lid to reveal a dozen bars of gold. Dooley raised himself up from his sitting position and studied the loot, wide-eyed.

'What is left after funding our rebellion, that is.'

'This is stolen property of the US government,' said Dooley, outraged.

'To whom do you think each cent's worth is more vital, the rich banker or the oppressed peasant?' pleaded Angel.

'You're suggesting it's there for the taking?' asked Dooley.

'*Be my guest.*'

There was a moment of tension as Dooley and Angel faced off to each other. Dooley looked at

Parker for support.

'Either way, was Rose Morrison's death justified?' asked Parker.

'Our bullets did not kill the woman,' said Angel. 'There were other men, hired guns, waiting on the rooftops. They killed her to damn me.'

'Who fired this shot?' asked Parker, taking the misshapen bullet from his pocket and holding it up to Angel.

'This is a mystery,' said Angel.

Again Dooley looked at Parker, who nodded. Both had the same name burned into their mind's eye. Bloody Bill Logan.

'Maybe not, Angel,' said Parker.

Parker was sure that Angel, or Tauro, was not a cold-blooded killer. Not a killer of innocent women anyway. Parker's warrant for Angel now seemed worthless, it was the last of the Regulators who should be returned to Terlingua in chains. Either that or buried in unmarked graves down Mexico way. Angel explained that Parker had arrived at an exciting time; his revolt against Ortega would reach its zenith tonight. Angel joked that after it, Tauro would become a legend and would grace the covers of his favourite dime novels.

'Like glorious lightning,' he said childishly, 'the brave Tauro drew his silver pistol and dispatched four of the evil General's henchmen!'

So he intended to assassinate Ortega. Probably walk right in to the wine cellar, draw his gun and fire without thought of the consequences, Parker thought. The kid was doomed, but Parker wasn't about to either aid him or try to dissuade him. Angel had chosen his destiny when he left the Hernandez ranch.

Parker used a dusty fragment of broken mirror to look over his split lip and busted tooth. He cleaned up the wound before joining the others around a fire for a meal of tortillas with meat and beans. At one point, the talk turned to Vasquez.

'He was a good man,' said Angel, who was now absurdly dressed in the khaki uniform of the captured soldier. 'But he was wet behind the ears, a romantic. Ortega was merciless.'

'How will you stop him, a dreamer like you?' asked Parker.

Angel thumbed the collar of the army uniform.

'Because this magic disguise cloaks all merciful thoughts.'

The manic sparkle in Angel's eyes sent a chill through Parker.

After the meal, Dooley sulked for the rest of the time at the hideaway. He found a secluded spot in the caverns and sat on a rock looking down into an apparently bottomless black pit. He had rolled up his shirtsleeves on account of the suffocating heat in the cave, and in his hand was the settler-child's doll with the yellow wool hair. Now he was quietly battling the overwhelming urge to just let the doll fall into the abyss. Dooley knew that Angel could be dead before the next sunrise. The kid seemed plain crazy to Dooley, though he wouldn't admit so much to Parker, who was his friend. There were not enough bullets in Mexico for the detective to take on an entire guerrilla army himself and snatch back the bank's remaining gold. When he left his office in New York he hadn't been prepared to fight Indians, bandits and bounty hunters. He envisaged a mystery fit for a gentleman sleuth, transplanted to a painted backdrop of the charmingly rugged frontier. Dooley now saw he was way off the mark and was beginning to wonder whether the bank's gold was worth his neck. He thought his next move through and came to the conclusion that he would wait until after the Ortega assassination. Should Angel somehow survive it, Dooley would then confront him with a demand for the gold or slap handcuffs on him, or take some such action. By then, Angel certainly would be guilty of murder. Having a plan, even a vague one, made Dooley feel a little comforted. Parker had wondered where Dooley had got to, and now walked over and sat nearby.

'How are you doing, Granville?' asked Parker.

Dooley sighed. 'The bank wanted their gold, but they also wanted Angel dead or alive,' he said.

'It figures.'

'I feel no better than Logan, a mercenary.'

'Don't put yourself down, Agent,' said Parker. 'If I didn't trust you, I wouldn't have let you come along.'

'But what chance do I have of seizing that gold back there?' asked Dooley.

'I don't think the poor of El Carricito will hand it back without another rebellion,' said Parker.

Dooley shook his head. 'Dime novel adventures,' he sighed.

Parker left the detective to his thoughts and sought out Angel on a tree-lined plateau above the dwellings. They spoke privately as the rebel leader prepared for his mission, looking uncomfortable in the uniform.

'Logan is out to kill us both,' said Parker. 'He's working for a rancher called Mulhearn, making raids on your father's hacienda.'

Angel seemed worried, then angry.

'And this *cabron* Logan is in El Carricito?' he asked.

'I think he killed Rose Morrison during the robbery,' said Parker. 'Now he's followed me down here, perhaps on Mulhearn's orders, to bury us and the truth.'

'I came here to protect my people, and abandoned my true blood-family,' said Angel.

'I'm also torn between my duty and my love for your family,' said Parker, sadly.

'For Inmaculada?'

Parker nodded, keeping his eyes on the ground.

'But now your duty is to punish Logan, no?' Angel continued.

'That's right.'

'At midnight when Ortega is dead, I will meet

you at the Mission San Juan,' said Angel. 'Then we will return to my father's *rancho* together.'

Parker nodded.

'I know that you really came here to protect me,' said Angel. Parker looked up and made eye contact as Angel squeezed his shoulder affectionately. 'Now *my* duty calls me to Ortega,' he continued.

ELEVEN

Just like a gathering thunderstorm, Angel's plan charged the air with electricity. Its momentum made Parker sick. He could do nothing but wait for murder to be committed. His own unenviable duty was to kill Logan, as a Ranger and as a father-less son. The lawmen rode out from the cave hide-away escorted by Paco a few hours before Angel planned to set out. The knowledge that Logan was waiting for a showdown in El Carricito enticed Parker back to the town as though it was written in the stars. Dooley, meanwhile, was figuring out how he could haul every hot carat back to Terlingua. He had agreed to back Parker up in the search for Logan, and to stand aside when they found him. But if anything happened to his friend, Dooley of course knew that he would have to continue the fight himself. His life and his sanity were on the line too.

The town was busy when the trio arrived, shaking off the numbing warmth of siesta. Paco said *'de nada'* when Parker apologized again for slugging him, then bid them farewell. Parker and Dooley returned to the hitching post behind the cantina to tether their steeds, then wandered among the town's locals searching for the Regulators. Parker saw how every corner of El Carricito was swarming with the sweat-stained khaki uniforms of Ortega's troops, and realized that Angel stood little chance of making it out alive. In Mexican, Parker thought, 'El Carricito' must mean suicide. They observed the saloons and hotels, the plaza and the bull-ring. Parker was fast losing his patience; he was itching to get some payback at Logan for pistol-whipping him. The idle troops were beginning to notice the two gringos. With Logan nowhere to be seen and the sun hanging low in the sky, Parker and Dooley retreated to the serene setting of the Mission San Juan.

Logan was riled by the way the two-bit general had been hoodwinked by a priest. The lawmen had been under his boot until divine intervention saved their skins, now he would have to stir up another opportunity. When Logan found out where Parker and Dooley had been arrested the previous night, he could scarcely believe the moronic *rurales* hadn't thought to follow through on the Tauro lead.

He had promised the envious Ortega the Sharps

rifle as a goodwill gesture and this had earned him an honorary captaincy. Of course Logan had no intention of parting with the heavily notched rifle and the rank meant less than the tin deputy stars dished out to a posse. It did, however, mean that Logan could use Ortega's expendables to wage war on Parker, Dooley and Angel, and get back across the Bravo to deal finally with Don Vicente. Along with Gray and the wounded Mulligan, Logan commandeered four armed troops and rode out to the adobe hut.

When the force arrived and stormed inside the little 'dobe with their guns cocked, the man named Paco was nowhere to be seen. Logan stared hard at the man's terrified mother and tapped the toe of his cowboy boot on the ground. It seemed to Gray that Bloody Bill's old brain took pedal-power to get working.

Logan acted soon enough though.

'All of you *pelados* get outside and set an ambush. I want him alive,' he barked. Logan whisked his Bowie knife out from its beaded Indian belt-sheath and stepped towards the old woman. When the rebel returned he would be forced to reveal the location of Angel's hideout. Then Logan would turn him over to the scavenger Mexicans like buzzard bait.

Seated in the pews of the Mission San Juan, Parker and Dooley were deep in conversation, discussing the intricacies of the case.

'I didn't come all this way to turn a blind eye to the robbers,' said Dooley, wiping his forehead with a handkerchief.

'Why should you have any loyalty for the bank?' asked Parker. 'Hell, it's government gold, it's insured isn't it? Angel's people have nothing.'

Parker didn't mean to sound as flippant as that. In fact, he understood exactly how Dooley felt.

'They're my clients. It's a matter of principle,' Dooley responded.

'Principles can get pretty flexible down here in the heat,' said Parker.

'Even yours?' asked Dooley, annoyed.

'Sure. I know when to bend the rulebook and give a loser a break,' Parker said. 'I also know when to come down on one like a blazing star stampede.'

'And Angel deserves a break?' asked Dooley.

'He's no loser. But his people deserve it,' said Parker.

Dooley thought for a moment.

'If I'm turning the other blind eye to an assassination,' he responded, 'then tonight Ortega ceases to be a thorn in anyone's side. Their little revolution will be over.'

'That doesn't end it,' said Parker. 'The bank don't expect their gold back, they want an assurance that Angel will be dealt with. Buchanan sends me after Angel, the bank hires you, and Mulhearn hires Logan to rub us all out. It's an insurance policy written in Rose Morrison's blood.'

Dooley sighed and hung his head. Parker was about to tell him, needlessly, that New York rules didn't apply down in Mexico, when a commotion from the plaza made them both look up. Parker walked over to the double arched doors of the church and opened one just enough to peer outside. Through the narrow gap he could see a group Ortega's men standing in the square, armed with their muzzle-loading muskets. An elderly woman dressed in black and with a shawl over her head was screaming and sobbing, holding her open arms up to the heavens. Parker could only make out a name that she repeated over and over again: '*Paco.*'

From the direction of Ortega's cellar, two *rurales* trooped a beaten man into the plaza, his head rolling back and forth like a sagging puppet. Parker had to squint a little to see his bruised face but there was no mistaking him as the man Parker had pistol-whipped. Logan and the two Regulators were there too, dressed in their dusters and watching the unfolding drama as entertainment. The old woman had ceased wailing and now clung to the semi-conscious Paco, trying in vain to free him from the guards. Parker edged forward when he saw the soldiers assemble in the line formation of a firing squad, but Dooley placed a protective hand on his shoulder. He noticed how the adobe wall against which the guards had propped Paco was already peppered with the bullet holes of earlier executions. Parker gripped the six-shooter by his side so tightly his knuckles had turned white.

'There's nothing you can do, Parker,' whispered Dooley. 'Let's wait for midnight and all hell to break loose.'

'Damn Ortega and damn Logan,' said Parker, enraged.

The old woman was silent in the few relentless seconds that followed. Blindfolded and with his hands tied behind him, Paco swayed against the wall as the soldiers levelled their muskets. It was Logan who barked the deadly order.

'*Fire!*'

A volley of smoky shots rolled along the line, Paco's squat body shuddering with each of the six bullet strikes. He dropped to the ground as though the puppet's strings had been cut right through. The soldiers and the Regulators saun- tered casually back to the cellar, leaving the dead man where he fell. Parker closed the door to muffle the sound of the old woman's screams.

'That's exactly what we'll do, Parker,' said Dooley. 'Damn them to hell.'

Parker hadn't caught the man's name before mistakenly pistol-whipping him last night. Of course now he knew it was Paco, short for Francisco, and he would probably never forget it either. Perhaps due to Parker's blunder the night before, Ortega's men had now interrogated and executed him. Parker didn't know whether to blame Angel's rebellion, the regime it was against, or his own stubborn pursuit of revenge dressed up as justice.

What Parker also didn't know was that Angel Hernandez had watched the execution with his own two eyes. Wearing the uniform disguise he had mingled with the troops as they left the square, a peaked cap pulled down over his eyes. Angel struggled to hold back tears of rage and guilt, sucking in the emotion and using it to demonize Ortega's face as he descended the steps to the cellar like the path down to hell. Now he felt the same fear as the soldier who had worn the uniform before. This was the stronghold of his enemy and he was outnumbered among them. Angel felt conscious that the sleeves of his jacket were a little short and the buttons strained by his broad frame. Then he saw how decadent and filthy the troops around him were and his nerves settled.

When a plump young woman collided with him, laughing, Angel grabbed the pewter tankard from her hand and drank deeply. Red wine soaked his jaw and dripped on to his boots. He wanted to numb his senses. Angel discreetly watched Ortega over the lip of the tilted tankard. The general was slumped in his throne in conversation with a man Angel assumed to be Logan, the man who was hounding his father. After a time, Ortega was seen to nod and give a sweeping wave of his hand before the Americans turned on their heels and marched back towards the steps. Angel prayed that Paco had not weakened in his hour of suffering.

In the silence of the church, Parker was hanging on every second for some sign of the assassination. He asked Dooley for the time when quiet had returned to the plaza. Dooley took out the gold pocket-watch by its chain and flipped the lid.

'Ten to midnight.'

'Angel will be here soon,' said Parker. 'He'll need my help.'

'In for a penny, in for a pound,' replied Dooley with a knowing smile.

They left the church to collect their saddle guns and ammunition from the horses. With those they could give Angel good covering fire when he came for Ortega at midnight. Parker and Dooley ran back across the empty plaza carrying the Spencer carbine and the Winchester rifle. Parker's mind was filled with questions: How close was the dead man to Angel? How long would his blood stain the wall as testament to that cold-blooded moment? How much longer would it stain Parker's conscience?

They were half-way across the square when the thunder of a hell-for-leather posse broke the still night. Parker stopped dead in his tracks and saw twenty of Ortega's men charge by on horseback. Bringing up the rear were three Anglos dressed in dusters. Logan and Parker made eye contact at exactly the same moment. Parker raised the carbine and Logan yanked the reins of his mount, breaking off from the posse. The other Regulators followed while the Mexican outfit continued unaware out of El Carricito.

'Bloody Bill Logan,' cried Parker as the thunder faded. 'I'm taking you in for the murder of Rose Morrison.'

Logan drew his six-shooter and answered with a bullet fired from the saddle. The shot went wide, though, and Parker countered with the carbine. Instantly he cocked the lever mechanism and fired again. He was shooting to kill now. Dooley had the other two Regulators covered with the Winchester, fanning the barrel between the two. He fired and put Gray down with a .44 round, spinning the man's half-holstered revolver towards the stars. Parker's second shot had struck Logan in the thigh and he struggled to stay aboard as his horse reared. Parker and Dooley darted for cover in different directions, Parker to the left and Dooley the right. They huddled down behind walls, aiming around the corners to the same target. Mulligan had joined the skirmish, blindly firing his six-shooter like a greenhorn by flip-cocking the hammer until its chamber was emptied. The bullets punched into the adobe wall beside Parker, scattering fragments of clay and straw. Parker worked the lever action on the carbine, calmly took aim and fired, knocking the hasty Regulator clean out of the saddle and into the dust.

'Crack shot, Parker!' he heard Dooley yelling.

Logan had steered his horse towards the door to the Mission San Juan and now slid out of the saddle. He slipped the Sharps rifle from its saddle boot as he hit the ground and fired from behind the frightened horse. A huge chunk of adobe brick exploded in front of Parker, blinding him for a moment. Parker rolled behind the wall and rubbed his gritty eyes, flinching when he heard the Sharps discharged again. Parker blinked until he could focus, then saw that Logan had retreated inside the church, its door just swinging shut. He looked across to Dooley's position and saw where the second round had hit home.

'Dooley!' he cried.

The detective was flat on his back and motionless. Parker checked the Regulators were out of action then broke cover and ran to him, lifting Dooley's head up slightly and noticing the glistening bullet wound in his chest. Dooley smiled when he saw Parker at his side. 'Dooley's Mexican Showdown . . .' he said weakly.

'I'm sorry Dooley, this wasn't meant to happen.'

'It was my case too.' The smile faded. 'The gold . . .' he whispered. 'It's your call, Parker.'

Dooley's mind was growing foggy and Parker's face was getting blurred. He was glad his new friend was beside him, but he wished he had the energy to take out his gold watch and look at Mary's picture.

Parker hesitated a moment after Dooley had slipped away. He fought back tears, biting down on his lip until it almost bled again, and then he headed to the Mission San Juan for his own show-down.

TWELVE

Angel only just caught sight of Parker marching inside the church, reloading his six-shooter as he went. He had ridden out from the shadows of an alleyway alongside the old wine-merchant building under which Ortega's thugs were squatting. Trembling with adrenaline and soiled with someone else's blood, he had come out behind the building and crept around to where a horse was tethered, ready for his getaway.

Dressed in that shabby and hated uniform he had blended in with the rowdy soldiers until, just before twelve, Ortega had retired to his private quarters with a sporting woman for the night. Following the sound of the woman's false laughter, Angel crept along the cobbled vaults of the vat chamber. Stepping through the puddles of stale wine, Angel drew a knife from under his tunic and slipped unseen and unheard into the gaudily decorated room located at the far end of the vault.

He could make out the flattering words of the woman now, lies to massage Ortega's ego. Angel caught sight of himself in a mirror with a gold frame and for the fleeting moment that it took to recognize himself in the uniform, his heart missed a beat. Angel's eyes darted from Ortega's broad back around the rich furnishings as he continued to step forward: oil-paintings of reclining beauties, gold ornaments and a lush fur rug to muffle Angel's footsteps.

The woman saw him first and froze, allowing Ortega to continue pawing her until Angel was close enough to touch. Angel looked into her big, dark eyes and saw a shared hatred for Ortega. As she saw the long knife-blade gleam, the woman thought how she would take Ortega's pesos when Angel was done, perhaps the gold ring from his fat finger too, then slink away into the night.

Angel touched the blade of the knife against the metal bedframe. It made the faintest of chink noises, but enough to alert Ortega to a third presence in the room. Angel allowed the general to see who had come for him before he sank the blade into the fancy uniform. As Angel withdrew the knife for the fifth and last time, a brass button from Ortega's jacket fell to the ground, speckled with blood.

Angel's heart was pounding so hard he felt it rise up into his throat. Looking down at the bloody knife in his hand, the situation dawned on him.

Ortega was dead.

Vasquez was avenged.

Tauro was legend.

He let the knife clatter to the ground and turned back to the door, wiping the blood from his hands on the army jacket. At the time he should have felt most like a man, Angel felt like doing nothing but weeping at his mother's grave.

The constant thunderclaps that rolled in over the plain towards the hacienda had nothing to do with atmospherics. They were gunshots. When Don Vicente pulled across the heavy velvet curtains and looked through the drawing-room window towards them, he could just make out the fleeting, random glow of muzzle-flash. The family had gathered in the room to await word of the attack from the chief ranch hand, Guillermo. Four of the cattle-ring's hired guns, Regulators, had ridden in with the twilight like nightrider ghouls, fixing to burn the *rancho* off the map. Their flaming torches had been spotted first by the ranch hands, just as they had before attacks on previous nights. The Anglos were always outgunned, but unlike Don Vicente's cowboys, they were professional killers. Don Vicente moved away from the window and rested a hand on his octogenarian mother's shoulder.

'Do not be scared, dear family,' he said. 'All that is right and good is here with us.' Dressed all in black, she sat with her head bowed and draped with a shawl, her eyes closed but twitching. It wasn't quite clear whether she was awake to hear her son's words of reassurance. In sharp contrast, Inmaculada sat across the room from her grand-mother, square-shouldered and with a defiant look on her youthful face. Her hair was pulled back tightly but rather than appearing severe, it made her look graceful. A cameo of Inmaculada's mother was pinned at her collar, and a crucifix hung from a long chain and rested at her bosom. Her only hint at nervousness was in the way her idle fingers fidgeted with the cross.

'Will that protect us, papa?' she said, making a statement as much as asking a question. Don Vicente's look was easy to read: *Only God knows.* He turned back to his desk and opened a small wooden box with brass lock and hinges. The lining was scarlet velvet and a Navy Colt revolver lay inside. Don Vicente looked down at it with distaste; he had hoped that toting a gun was behind him, part of another life. As he ran a finger along the engraved barrel, Don Vicente was startled by the door to the drawing-room opening. Guillermo staggered breathless inside, clutching a wound on his upper right arm.

'Don Vicente,' he gasped, 'the men are tired and wounded, we cannot keep the Regulators back all night.'

Don Vicente lifted the revolver from the case. He was already heading over to the window when

138

he spoke defiantly, 'Do you suggest we die?'

Guillermo watched as Don Vicente smashed one of the small square panes of glass with the barrel of the Colt.

'We will defend the hacienda until our last bullet is fired,' said Don Vicente, looking at his own inky reflection in the unbroken panes. When a figure dressed in a long duster moved in the darkness, *El Monje* fired his first bullet.

For a man of God, Father Octavio Perez had little patience. He kept shifting position in his hiding-place behind a rock, looking down at the meandering valley path far below. The heavy cap-and-ball revolvers in each of the priest's hands were ice cold and made his fingers numb. Under a bright crescent moon, Perez considered his situation: priest or bandit?

Whatever his role, he had just set the hogleg pistols down on the rocks by his feet and was flexing his tingling hands when the signal came. It was the squawk of a bird, mimicked by one of the guerrillas further down the path, and it meant Ortega's cavalry were coming their way. The first Perez saw of them was a moonlit dust cloud accompanied by the thundering of galloping hoofs. The posse was big, perhaps twenty horses and their riders. The ambush was set to catch them in a turkey-shoot, which Perez thought a shame as those twenty fine steeds, God's creatures, would be shot all to hell too. Perez reasoned with himself that the troops were on the way to massacre the cave-dwellers and loot the looted gold.

The posse was half-way across the canyon floor when the first shot rang out. That was the second signal, the trigger for the attack. As Perez peered over the edge of the rock he could feel and taste the updraught of dust disturbed by the charging horses. He selected one of the anonymous khaki bodies as a target and fired off the percussion cap with a crack of sparks and smoke. The other guerrillas had acted on the signal too. They stuck their heads up like prairie gophers and fired a barrage of lead down into the valley. Horses whinnied and reared up, tossing their riders into the dust to be trampled or plugged; some were dead before they had even left the saddle. As he squeezed the triggers, Perez's thoughts were dominated by one question.

Priest or bandit . . . ?

He had hit two men square in their backs, enough to kill them both for sure. That was his duty done. The others reloaded and began again, until the only movement on the canyon floor was the debris kicked up by rounds ploughing into the dirt. Gradually, one by one, the barrage waned to a single, last shot that struck a dead man. As the smoke cleared and the carnage became clear, the guerrillas began to whoop and holler, tossing their sombreros into the air and firing off the last of their rounds after them.

Perez was grim-faced. Was he a priest or a bandit for his part in this massacre? Tauro would say that it was God's work to drive these demons from Mexico. Perez tucked the smoking revolvers into his sash belt. '*Amen*,' he whispered, flexing his numb trigger finger.

When Parker stepped inside the church, he was driven by something far darker than his sense of justice or desire to avenge his father. He was a steam-engine fuelled by hatred, there to end Logan's existence; he could almost hear Rose and Dooley goading him on. Parker's footsteps echoed on the stone floor of the church as he walked towards the altar. The silence and heat inside the church seemed to weigh down upon Parker's shoulders; he blinked his eyes to focus. He carefully laid the carbine on a pew as he passed by it, without slowing or shifting his gaze from the shrine ahead. The free hand now drifted up to his *buscadero* holster where it settled on the six-shooter, drawing it and cocking the hammer. The revolver felt good there, like an extension of his forearm.

'Logan?'

The Sharps rifle blasted a response immediately, cracking open a stone baptism-font. Logan had been waiting to fire that shot, just as he had for Joseph. Parker ducked and aimed the six-shooter towards the shadows of the sacristy, squeezing off a shot. As the echoes and powder smoke drifted slowly up to the rafters, Parker listened for signs of life, his ears ringing. He recocked the hammer and side-stepped closer to the altar, watching and waiting.

Logan stepped out from cover and fired again, before moving quickly behind a wooden pillar. The round struck another post to Parker's left, sending wood splinters into his face.

'You killed her, didn't you Logan,' Parker called out. 'Didn't you.'

Parker heard a burst of croaky laughter from behind the post.

'Mulhearn's paying me to give you a wood suit too, junior,' came the response. 'Father and son alike.'

'That's what *you*'ve got coming, Logan,' said Parker bitterly. 'A generation late.' Parker saw the Sharps rifle move from behind the pillar. He edged slightly back towards the door of the church until the sleeve of Logan's duster was visible.

'Was it an accident, Logan?' asked Parker as he moved. 'Crossfire? Or was it all done to frame Angel as her killer?'

'Accident nothing,' barked Logan. 'Fellas in the chips, like Mulhearn and the mayor, pay me to get bloody on their behalf. That's why they call me Bloody Bill, see.'

Parker thought of Buchanan, remembering how he had taken an instant dislike to him at the barbershop. Parker could see that Logan was readying the Sharps for another shot.

'It was like shooting nothing, truth be told,' continued Logan. 'I see her dying and couldn't help but feel *stimulated*. I'm awful easy on the trigger, just ask your old man when you see him.'

Logan's words speeded up a fraction towards the end of the intentionally incendiary statement. He began to swing around the side of the pillar to aim the rifle when Parker made his move. Running back towards the door with his head low, Parker fired his six-shooter from the hip and fanned the hammer until five rounds had been discharged in rapid succession. Logan had ducked away before the first bullet hit home, all of Parker's .44 rounds punching into the pillar that shielded him. Logan had counted the burst of gunfire that came his way: five rounds plus the one fired earlier, he made it. The Ranger had let red-eyed anger cloud his good sense. Shoot low and wound him, Logan thought, then get up close and look into his eyes as he expires.

'It'll be like *that* when my boys do for Angel's sister,' said Logan. 'Immaculate, is she?'

Parker absorbed the taunts, waiting for his time to come. Logan was smiling as he stepped around the pillar, levelling the barrel of the Sharps rifle with his finger closing on the trigger. There was just enough time for his smile to fade when he saw Parker.

When Parker's fifth and final shot had cleared the barrel of the six-shooter he was level with the

pew on which the carbine rested. He let the
revolver fall from his hand; it went spinning empty
across the floor of the church towards the door.
With a twist of his body he had retrieved the
carbine and worked the lever action to prepare it
for the last shot he intended to fire. And then
came the frozen moment, a mere split second of
time when Logan stood grim faced and speechless,
and Parker's trigger finger curled inwards.

The carbine's blast ended that lull, even ringing
out in the bell-tower high above. The man-stop-
ping round hit Logan in the right side of his chest,
spinning him back around the pillar. The Sharps
rifle clattered to the ground and 'Bloody' Bill
stumbled over it towards the altar, dripping blood
in a slug's trail. Parker cocked the lever on the
carbine again and took slow steps after the dying
bounty hunter. Logan fell on to the steps at the
foot of the altar and rolled around to face his foe.
He exhaled, knowing this time he had been
beaten. Parker's left hand moved away from the
barrel of the carbine and up to his jacket pocket. It
returned with the old bullet from the porch of the
bank. Parker threw it down on to Logan's chest
where it bounced and came to rest on the ground.
The eyes of both men were on the small but signif-
icant object.

'You fired that bullet back in Terlingua,' said
Parker. 'Only now does it hit its mark.'

Logan's hand was weakly reaching for the
revolver in his belt. Parker raised the carbine and

stepped towards Logan, leaning in to draw the six-shooter from his holster. He straightened up and aimed the revolver down at its owner. The doors to the church creaked open and Parker turned to look over his shoulder. Angel stood in the doorway, dressed in the bloodstained army uniform. He took a few steps inside as Parker heard Logan's weak voice.

'Parker . . .' he whispered.

Parker turned his attention back to Logan. He was near death but smiling deviously.

'Sha-llo-water,' he whispered slowly, like the word was a weapon.

Angel watched as Parker cocked the hammer of the six-shooter and fired once into the man on the steps.

He had been there that day, watching and waiting. Hidden on the rooftop of the billiard-hall, Logan and his Regulators witnessed Angel and his four men ride into Terlingua. The street was empty as the Mexicans dismounted and headed for the bank on foot. Logan had to tug on the sleeve of one hair-trigger bounty hunter who was ready to open fire.

'Not until they're back out,' Logan had said. '*Then* they're thieves.'

And they had waited. Logan's sweating hands caressed his rifle, he licked his lips and squinted his eyes. Movement was visible through the bank's window for a few long minutes before the little bell above the bank-door chimed.

Logan moved quickly, taking aim and firing the opening shot towards Angel as he calmly came out of the bank carrying a sack. The heavy-calibre Sharps round burrowed into a wooden post and Logan cussed as Angel ran as fast as the loot would allow him. That shot unleashed chaos in the sleepy street, the confused Mexicans returning fire in all directions. As the robbers mounted up and attempted an escape, one horse stopped a bullet from the Regulators and collapsed to the ground, trapping its rider.

Through the chaos, almost frozen still like a photograph, Logan saw *her*. Rose Morrison, a prim blonde, dropped the schoolbooks she was carrying, hitched up her skirt-hem and ran across the street towards the firing-zone. The boy with tin star and wooden pistol watched her too, jaw slack in wonder at the real, live gunfight.

'Let 'em go,' Logan said suddenly, the wicked glint of a conspiracy in his eye.

'*What?*'

The Mexicans thundered out of town and Rose scurried gracefully towards the fallen bandit, her lace-up leather boots leaving dainty footsteps in the dust road. She looked down at the struggling Mexican, at the six-shooter in his hand, before backing away towards the bank. Logan had a better way to blacken the Hernandez name. He squinted one eye and peered down the sight of his Sharps rifle, then he fired. The shot broke the returning silence. Rose Morrison toppled to the ground, the speckled pattern of her bodice and the fingers of her gloves wet with spilled blood. The pages of Rose's discarded schoolbooks fluttered in a light breeze as Logan casually spat a brown wad of tobacco on the rooftop.

'There you go, Mulhearn.'

THIRTEEN

The plaza was eerily quiet when Parker and Angel stepped out from the Mission San Juan. The horses hadn't moved since Parker last saw them, neither had their dead riders, Mulligan and Gray. Dooley was there at the far corner of the square, somehow Parker had hoped he'd gotten up and dusted himself off in his typical way. Parker walked over and gently hoisted the body up on to his shoulder, carrying it towards the hitching post where his horse had been tethered earlier.

Angel commandeered Dooley's appaloosa horse, the one paid for by the bank, which he deemed better than the crow bait intended for his getaway. Parker carried the detective's body over the saddle in front of him, the dead man's head and boots hanging down towards the ground. When they rode back out into the plaza a few minutes later, they heard a hullabaloo coming from the wine-merchant's building. Ortega's murder had been discovered and the alarm was being raised.

Dooley's body weighed heavy on Parker's saddle and his conscience as they travelled into the night. This time, Parker did not look back at El Carricito.

A few short hours after the San Juan showdown, Parker buried Dooley. He had fashioned a wooden cross as best he could and it now stood at the head of the grave-mound bearing a carved inscription:

AGENT GRANVILLE 'WYATT' DOOLEY
PINKERTONIAN

Parker stood there a while, silently. He knew the establishment wouldn't get what they wanted on this crossing. The gold would be lost, Angel would go free, and Parker himself wasn't prepared to whitewash the corruption under the rock that was the Terlingua gentlemen's club. Torn between two masters, between two faces of the law, Parker knew he'd be stripped of his star. But first he would take his brand of justice to them.

Angel led them to a derelict *cabaña* shack that now barely stood upright. It was, however, ideal for keeping your head down, Parker observed. Perez would soon meet them here with news of the ambush.

Angel had removed his military tunic and was now just wearing the stripe-legged trousers, boots and pouch belt with a dirty white shirt. He and Parker sat inside the shack, having tethered their horses in an enclosure at the back. Parker, dressed in his shirtsleeves, was wearing Dooley's shoulder holster and Remington revolver.

'Francisco tipped Ortega's men off to a bogus hideout before he was executed,' said Angel. 'We knew to set an ambush there for them. God willing, those dogs will have been massacred.'

'Then Ortega's rule has been crushed?' asked Parker.

'*Sí*, with Ortega dead in his bed, his surviving thugs have lost their power.'

'Then Tauro is free to return to the hacienda, as he said he would?' asked Parker.

Angel smiled and nodded his head.

'I have grown to become a man of my word, you see Parker,' he answered.

Parker nodded that he knew as much already.

'But ... it is clear I cannot stay for ever,' he added. 'I was not guilty of killing the teacher, but the robbery I hold my hands up to gladly. Not all *norteamericanos* will be as forgiving or as sympathetic as you.'

'You'll return to Mexico?' asked Parker.

'It is my home,' Angel said with a proud smile. 'Tell me, *amigo*, did you really believe that I was guilty of the teacher's murder?'

'Not for a second,' replied Parker, not entirely convincingly.

Father Perez, the bandit padre, arrived at dawn. He had ridden to the *cabaña* on an old, open prairie wagon drawn by a *burro*. When he saw Angel, he could hardly contain his excitement.

'You did the impossible, *compadre*!' he enthused. 'You've slain that devil Ortega in his own lair . . . in his own bed!'

'What of the ambush? Was it a success?' asked Angel, trying in vain to subdue the priest.

'The raiders were defeated, we suffered no casualties,' said Perez, 'and word from El Carricito is that Ortega's gang have scattered in confusion.'

'*Bueno*,' said Angel. 'And the gold?'

'I have it here,' replied Perez, pointing to the treasure-box in the back of the wagon. 'To be distributed to the Church . . . and to the poor.'

Parker was cynical, his eyes narrowing. He would have to use some imagination in the writing of his report.

Father Perez rode away into the first light of dawn, shouting '*Vaya con Dios*' over his shoulder. It meant 'Go with God.' Parker had said nothing about the gold before the padre left, and would not mention it again this side of the border. He and Angel remained at the shack long enough to tend their horses and brew coffee for breakfast, before mounting up and riding out towards the border.

Both Parker and Angel had the spirit to go the extra mile now, pushing themselves and their horses to their limits. The lives of the innocents depended on it. The hacienda called out from across the expanse of territory that separated them. For Angel, it found wings in the voice of his late mother, begging him to reconcile with Don Vicente; for Parker it was in the sweet ballads of Inmaculada. Bill Logan was dead, as was his Mexican outfit. But other Regulators survived in Terlingua, the hired guns of greedy millionaire Theodore Mulhearn. It was he, ultimately, who must answer to the law if any harm came to Parker's spiritual kinfolk. It scared Parker that the same image was no doubt in Angel's mind, the same scene with the slight differences of a parallel world. *Did the same thought in two minds make it real,* he wondered. He tried to think of nothing but a white wall of light to block out that terrible thought, but wave after wave of ugly reality hounded him.

That was how the journey passed, the American and the Mexican side by side. They rode among the bones of cattle picked clean by scavengers, through a familiar land that seemed more impos-ing to Parker now. The hills ahead of them were like the sloping waves of an ocean, shimmering with heat haze and faded by the sun to the same bleached white of the sky. They saw no Comanche though the threat of attack seemed to hang over them like a shadow. Only when their horses were lathered with sweat did they bother to stop of a night, bedding down in the abandoned *ranchos* that were scattered over the landscape.

A night and a day later, the tortuous pattern of the return journey was broken when Angel's horse stumbled on cholla cactus and pitched forward into the dust. Angel fell heavily and rolled clear of the horse, shaking himself down and checking for injuries but finding none. Parker yanked the reins in his hand and brought his own horse around. He got down off his mount and walked towards the fallen horse. Kneeling at its side, he patted its neck and examined its front legs. The wounded horse was struggling weakly to get back upright. Parker began to check the saddle-bags for salvageable goods. Under the flap of the exposed saddle-bag, Parker found the little doll with the yellow wool hair. He held it firmly in his hand for a moment before taking it with him back to his own horse. Parker took time to meticulously stow the supplies in his own saddle rig, then turned back to the wounded horse. Angel watched as he drew the Remington from the hideout holster and aimed it at the horse's head. The gunshot cracked and echoed across the landscape, its smoke cloud carried instantly away by the breeze.

They rode double and for a while Parker was silent, bothered by having had to put Dooley's fine horse to sleep. The sentiment faded when they stumbled upon a small overnight camp. It wasn't done to cut straight through uninvited, so Parker hollered to one of the men he saw who was saddling a horse.

'Howdy,' he yelled. The cowboy turned and took a few steps towards the horse with two riders. His hand was firmly on the walnut handle of his holstered revolver.

'Can I help you?' he asked.

'Just passing through to Terlingua from across the Bravo,' said Parker, casually. 'Any news worth reading about?'

'I dunno,' the cowboy answered nervously. He craned his neck forward and raised his chin to study the strangers. 'That pepper-gut back there a prisoner?' He was meaning Angel.

'Why, you . . .' Angel began to protest until Parker nudged him back in the saddle.

'No, he's no prisoner,' said Parker. 'We're headed for Casa Hernandez, few miles that-a-way.'

Parker looked around the camp and saw a second horse grazing on the fringe.

'You alone, partner?' he asked, his eyes on the second horse.

'Sure.'

Parker noted the man's sudden nervousness. He looked at the camp-fire twenty feet away and saw a second cowboy on the ground near it; though he was obscured by scrub bushes it was possible to see the man had a head wound. He was draped with a buff coloured blanket. Parker focused on it . . . not a blanket . . . a duster coat.

The Regulator made a move to draw his revolver and Parker caught the jerk of the man's elbow out of the corner of his eye. He drew lightning fast and fired from the hip, grazing the man's gun hand and sending the revolver itself flying off into the dust. The Regulator screamed and his buddy muttered, delirious. So the remaining Regulators *had* laid siege to Don Vicente's

154

ranch, and blood *had* been shed.

When the gunshot echo and the disturbed neighs of the three horses had abated, only the Regulator's pained groans were heard. He was doubled up, gripping his wounded hand and cussing at Parker.

'What trouble have you brought on the Hernandez family?' asked Parker, apprehensively.

'We r–raided them, in the end they f–fought us back, ain't no Hernandez hurt, honest. We needed Bloody Bill with us, see.'

'Logan's dead, I shot him for the killing of Miss Rose.'

The Regulator looked shocked.

'Unless you want a second bullet I suggest you ride out with your partner there and find yourselves another boss.'

The Regulator didn't waste any time. He hoisted his semi-conscious buddy into the saddle of his horse and tied his legs to the stirrups. Then he mounted his own steed, looked north in the direction of Terlingua and the Hernandez ranch, and promptly rode off westward towards Redford.

'Some people don't deserve mercy, but I guess that's not for us to decide,' said Angel bitterly.

Parker watched the wounded Regulators go, wondering if either man had witnessed the murder of Rose Morrison. He hoped it was the last he would see of the Regulators, a corrupt private army just like Ortega's *rurales*. When he was sure they were gone, Parker spurred the horse onwards.

*

They followed the Terlingua creek until the Hernandez ranch came into view. To the naked eye it seemed tranquil and beautiful on the horizon, a haven of warmth and compassion set in an unfriendly landscape. Parker took out his telescope lens and looked again. Now he could see the facts: ranch hands patrolling on horseback and carrying rifles, half a dozen man-size bundles stacked up beside a corral fence, the blackened mess of an extinguished fire blighting a portion of the hacienda's front wall.

'What do you see?' Angel asked over Parker's shoulder.

'Echoes of that raid that was fought off last night,' he replied. 'Some unburied dead. Your father's men are in control now.'

'Let us see for sure,' urged Angel.

Parker closed the lens and drove his horse on towards the ranch. When the exhausted cowboys spotted the distant strangers coming at them, they rallied and cocked their weapons for another shoot-out. Both Parker and Angel were familiar faces, though, and when they got up close the most eagle-eyed of them cried out Angel's name and the pair were met with cheers of celebration. Any sense of danger was forgotten as Angel slipped from the saddle and was promptly hoisted, grinning, on to the shoulders of the ranch hands. The ranch boss Guillermo was thanking God for the heir's return, his arm in a sling and a patch of red soaking through the white bandage.

Ain't no Hernandez hurt, honest. That was the Regulator's version of it anyway. Parker was nevertheless scanning the windows of the hacienda for signs of life when the excitement reached the ears of those inside. The front door opened and out rushed Inmaculada with Esperanza, her pink-silk dress flowing around her. Don Vicente and even old Marshal McOwen followed her out. *Thank God*, thought Parker. Angel saw them too, quickly gesturing to be lowered to his feet. He cut through the crowd of ranch hands and embraced his tearful sisters, then turned to his father. Don Vicente's forehead was blackened and bleeding slightly. He appeared to have helped put out the recent fire.

'What have they done to you, Father?' he asked.

'They came night after night, relentlessly. We defended our home from them,' said Don Vicente proudly. 'The *hombres* who wore the long coats are gone now. Mulhearn and his cattle-ring can never destroy *this*.' Don Vicente looked around him at his family.

Parker reached into his saddle-bag and took out the little settler child's doll, holding it out for Esperanza who was in Inmaculada's arms. Parker smiled and broke off adoring eye-contact with Inmaculada.

'Rose Morrison's killer is belly-up too, Walt,' he said to the marshal. 'It was Bloody Bill.'

*

157

While the ranch hands chose a new palomino horse for Parker and saddled it with his kit, Parker wandered out on to the veranda where Marshal McOwen smoked his pipe and rocked gently on the hanging chair outside the hacienda. Parker rested against the spindles of the porch front and felt the sun against the back of his neck. He drew Dooley's Remington and checked the rounds in the chamber. Inmaculada was seated in a rocking-chair at the far end of the veranda, cooling herself with a semicircular fan. Alongside her a canary chirped in a cage. When she saw the gun, Inmaculada stood and walked away, offended. Parker reholstered the gun in the shoulder rig and made eye-contact with McOwen.

'You look like you're set for a showdown,' said Marshal McOwen apprehensively. 'Logan's not the end of it, huh?'

Parker shook his head, straightening up. 'Theodore Mulhearn is.'

Parker wandered out into the grounds behind the hacienda. He saw Inmaculada by her mother's grave, a pretty parasol shielding her from the sun. She noticed him approaching and began twirling the parasol on her shoulder.

'You must go soon ... with your guns?' she asked.

Parker nodded, hurt by his own broken promise. 'The case isn't through yet.'

'You will take care. We would like very much to see you here again, my father is most fond of you.

158

As we all are.' She was nervous, avoiding eye-contact. 'I know all that happened. I cannot thank you enough for the way you helped Angel. It will bring you trouble that you did not follow orders?'

'If it does, then the star doesn't stand for what I thought it did,' he replied.

'Did you care for her, the woman who died?' she asked.

'Miss Rose? I never met her.'

'But she was in your thoughts while you were in Mexico?'

Parker looked at Inmaculada and thought. 'No, not her.'

She began to cry and quickly turned to leave. Before walking away towards the hacienda under the shade of the parasol, she leaned towards Parker and kissed him on the cheek.

'*Adios,* Parker.'